CINDERELLA'S ROYAL SEDUCTION

CINDERELLA'S ROYAL SEDUCTION

DANI COLLINS

MILLS & BOON

First published in Great Britain 2020
by Mills & Boon, an imprint of HarperCollins*Publishers*
1 London Bridge Street, London, SE1 9GF

Large Print edition 2020

© 2020 Dani Collins

ISBN: 978-0-263-08458-0

MIX
Paper from
responsible sources
FSC C007454

This book is produced from independently certified
FSC™ paper to ensure responsible forest management. For
more information visit www.harpercollins.co.uk/green.

Printed and bound in Great Britain
by CPI Group (UK) Ltd, Croydon, CR0 4YY

My long-suffering family always deserves a dedication for cheerleading me in this career I've chosen, but when it comes to the nuts and bolts of actually getting a book written there are two people I absolutely cannot do without.

First and foremost, my editor. I've been lucky enough to work with Laurie Johnson on and off in the seven years I've been published. Thank you for helping me turn so many pumpkins into carriages, this book very much included.

Second and no less important, my RMT, Loretta. Thank you for keeping the carpal tunnel and shoulder gremlins at bay, for being a fan of romance, and for recommending I visit Sparkling Hills in Vernon, the spa that inspired the one in this book.

PROLOGUE

JUST ONCE, CASSIOPEIA BRODEUR wished she could be given enough time to sit and think before having to react to whatever catastrophe her stepmother, Maude, had set in motion.

She really wished that when she'd been fifteen and thinking she was welcoming her stepsisters into her family, she hadn't told them her friends called her Sopi.

"Soapy?" Nanette and Fernanda spoke English as their fourth language, but they'd heard the pun and laughed hysterically.

Seven years later, all of Sopi's childhood friends, including the ones who'd given her the nickname when they'd been in grade school, had moved on to university and world travel, interesting jobs and serious relationships and *cities.*

While Sopi was still here in Lonely Lake, scrubbing up after her spoiled stepfamily and the guests of the hotel and spa that bore her name.

Why couldn't Maude and the girls shove off back to Europe and quit destroying what was left of her life? They certainly made no effort to hide their disdain for this "backwater village" in the remote wilderness of the Canadian Rockies.

Oh, right, they had run through all of Sopi's father's money and had nowhere left to turn. Yet they seemed determined to drive this place into ruin, too.

"*All* the reservations?" Sopi repeated with disbelief. "You canceled *all* of March?"

"Yes."

"On purpose?"

"Sopi." Maude used her most hideously patronizing tone. "We can't have families with children running around when we're entertaining royalty, can we? And we'll need the rooms."

"Royalty?" Sopi asked with a choke of hysterical laughter. "Is that a figure of speech?" The odd aging pop star turned up—emphasis on *odd*—but real celebrities with real money went to Banff or Whistler for their spring skiing.

"Rhys Charlemaine is the prince of Verina."

"Never heard of him," Sopi said flatly, even though it rang a distant bell. She barely had time to keep up with weather reports and the latest safety regulations, though. She didn't follow gossip on fading royalty.

"Honestly, Sopi. Your lack of education." Maude shook her coiffed silver head in despair.

Was she referring to the education that hadn't been paid for because instead Sopi's father's money had been used to keep Nanette and Fernanda in boarding school in Switzerland? The girls' absence had turned out to be a blessing, so Sopi didn't complain much about it, but honestly.

"Why on earth would a prince come here?" Sopi asked.

"Because I've arranged a week of heli-skiing for him."

With what money?

Sopi wanted to scream or maybe cry. She glanced longingly beyond the windows where

February skies were an intense blue over blinding white slopes across the valley. Last season, she'd skied once on the small commercial hill on the far side of the lake. This year she hadn't had a single opportunity—too busy trying to keep the spa afloat.

"And as for the accommodation," Maude continued absently, "the girls will move from the penthouse so he can use it, but they'll stay on the top floor. His entourage will take the rest of the rooms there."

"His *entourage*? Please tell me this isn't *all* complimentary." Sopi knew it would be and felt sick. Sick. Maude never let her peek at the books, but Sopi wasn't blind or stupid. She knew they were in the red and bleeding more every day.

"Of course we won't charge him." Maude's scoffing tone chided her as Silly Sopi. "This is exceedingly good exposure for us. Everyone will want to come here, especially while he's in residence. I've arranged a decent chef. That's long overdue." Her pointed look blamed Sopi for not having made that happen sooner, and Sopi couldn't even imagine what it was going to cost. "You'll need to hire more staff for the treatments."

"Maude." Sopi tried one more time, even though this argument had never made an impact. "There is no one to hire."

The occasional adventurous cosmetician or massage therapist joined them for a season, but the isolation of Lonely Lake wasn't for everyone. Plus, Maude and her daughters were a special kind of hell to work for. Their incessant demands and tantrums over inconveniences like having to wait for deliveries of a desired shade of nail polish impacted the spa's ability to retain qualified employees.

"You always make things harder than they are," Maude sighed. "People will beg to work for gratuities if you tell them who will be staying here."

The spa's bread-and-butter clientele were retirees soaking their arthritis in the hot mineral pools at an affordable price. Sopi couldn't deny that a high-profile guest would fill rooms, but, "Seniors on fixed incomes aren't known for their generous tips. If this prince and his cronies—"

"Cronies?" Maude's head came up. "Sopi,

he's *thirty*. Unmarried. And it's time he changed that." Maude had been fingering through a collection of fabric swatches. She held up a square of cranberry silk. "Would this clash with Nanette's hair, do you think?"

As was often the case when Sopi spoke with her stepmother, Sopi's brain was racing to catch up. Even as she tried to formulate arguments against whatever Maude was demanding, she knew the struggle was futile. Her stepmother had gained control of the spa when Sopi's father died and kept a firm grasp on it. Sopi didn't have the resources to fight her for it, and Maude would no doubt clean out what was left of the spa's available cash to repulse an attack. Sopi would be bankrupt whether she won or lost.

Sopi's only choice was to try to keep the place solvent until she had enough in her savings account to mount a proper legal challenge. Maybe it was a fool's dream, but it kept her going.

So she was always mentally planning how to mitigate or adapt to or accomplish whatever ridiculous thing Maude insisted had to happen while doing the math, trying to calculate when she would be able to put her foot down and hold her ground.

Today, amid that familiar scramble, Sopi's brain crashed into Maude's end goal. Maude wanted to marry one of her daughters to a prince. To a man who lived in a kingdom—or was it a principality? Who cared? It was far, far away.

If one left, they all would.

A tentative ray of hope gleamed like a beacon at the end of a long, dark tunnel, breaking a smile across Sopi's face.

"You know what, Maude? You're right. This sounds like a tremendous opportunity. I'll start prepping for it." Sopi's pulse pounded so hard, her ears rang.

"Thank you," Maude said in a beleaguered tone that echoed with, *It's about time.* "Leave moving the girls out of the penthouse until the last moment. They don't want to be inconvenienced any more than necessary."

Sopi nearly choked on her tongue, but she bit down on it instead. If she played her cards right, and if she threw her stepsisters in front of this Prince Charlemaine or whoever the heck he was, then maybe, just maybe, she could free herself of her stepfamily forever.

It was such an exciting prospect, she hummed cheerfully as she left Maude's office and headed upstairs to strip beds and clean toilets.

CHAPTER ONE

RHYS CHARLEMAINE WOKE before the sun was up. Before any of his staff began creeping into his suite with fresh coffee and headlines and messages that required responses.

He didn't ring for any of them. What privacy he had was precious. Plus, he had withstood enough bustle and fussing yesterday when he and his small army of assistants, bodyguards and companions had arrived. The owner of this place, Maude Brodeur, had insisted on personally welcoming him. She had hung around for nearly two hours, dropping names and reminiscing about her first husband, whom she had cast as a contemporary equal to Rhys's father—which he wasn't. He had been a distant cousin to a British earl and largely unknown.

Blue blood was blue blood, however, and she had clearly been using the association to frame her pretty, well-educated daughters as suitable for a man next in line to a throne. Her daughters had perched quietly while she rattled on, but there'd been an opportunistic light in their eyes.

Rhys sighed. If he had a euro for every woman who wanted to search his pockets for a wedding ring, he would have more money than all the world's tech billionaires combined.

Instead, he had a decent fortune built on shrewd investments, some of it in tech, but much of it in real estate development. Half of it belonged to his brother, Henrik. Rhys handled their private interests while Henrik looked after the throne's finances. They each had their lane, but they drove them side by side, always protecting the other's flank. Rhys might be the spare, a prince to his brother the king, but they were a solid unit.

Even so, he and Henrik didn't always agree. This detour to a tiny off-grid village in Canada had had his brother lifting his brows with skepticism. "Sounds too good to be true," had been Henrik's assessment.

Rhys's antennae were up, as well. On the surface, the property in a valley reminiscent of Verina's surrounding Alps appeared ripe for exploitation, especially with its hot-spring aquifer. That alone made it a unique energy opportunity. The remote location would be a challenge, of course, but there was a modest ski hill across the lake. It drew locals and guests of this hotel, but could also be picked up for a song and further developed.

Maude was claiming she wanted to keep the sale of the spa quiet for "personal reasons," pretending she didn't need the money. Normally, Rhys would steer clear of someone attempting to pull the wool over his eyes. He had his own reason for accepting her invitation, however, and it had nothing to do with whether or not this place was a sound investment.

Rhys shifted his pensive gaze across the frozen lake, searching for answers that couldn't be solved with money and power. He needed a miracle, something he didn't believe in. He was a man of action who made his own destiny, but the only action available to him at the moment was a path littered with disloyalty to his brother, if not the crown.

He supposed he should be thankful the doctors had finally discovered the reason Henrik and his wife, Elise, were failing to conceive. They'd caught Henrik's testicular cancer early enough that treatment had a reasonable chance of success. With luck, Rhys would not assume the throne. Not soon, at any rate, but Henrik would almost certainly be sterile.

That meant the task of producing future progeny to inherit the throne had fallen into Rhys's lap.

Which meant he needed a wife.

He tried not to dwell on how treasonous that felt. Henrik had worked tirelessly to regain their rightful place in Verina. Doing so had nearly cost him the woman he loved. The royalists who had supported their return from exile had expected Henrik to marry an aristocrat, not a diplomat's daughter. Somehow, Henrik had overcome their objections only to come up against the inability to make an heir.

Henrik and Elise deserved children. They would be excellent parents. Given everything Henrik had gone through, the throne ought to go to his child, not Rhys's.

None of this felt right to him.

A blue glow came on below his window,

dragging Rhys out of his brooding. The lights in the free-form mineral bath illuminated the mist rising off the placid water, beckoning him.

His security detail had reported that the guest register was swollen with female names, many of them bearing titles or related to one. He wasn't surprised his intention to ski here had been leaked to the press, drawing the usual suspects. He had counted on Maude being canny enough to see the value in a full house. It made the place look successful and ensured she would still have a nice influx of cash even if he turned down her offer to purchase. She might even have thought a bevy of beautiful naked women would sway him to buy.

It wouldn't, but he appreciated the expediency of having a curated selection of eligible women brought to one place for his consideration.

He had no choice but to marry and was down to his last moments of bachelorhood. He decided to make the most of them. He dropped the pajama pants he'd slipped on when he rose and left them on the floor, mostly to reassure his staff that he hadn't been kidnapped. He'd learned to pick up after himself during his years in exile with his brother. He was a passable cook and could trim his own beard, not that he did those things for himself anymore.

He was a prince again, one who had believed his primary function was to ensure his family's economic viability while his brother ruled their country and provided heirs. His responsibilities were expanding, though, and the one duty he would happily perform— taking his brother's place while he battled his illness—was not open to him.

Heart heavy, he shrugged on his monogrammed robe, stepped into his custom-sewn slippers, searched out the all-access card Maude had given him, then took the elevator to the treatment level.

Sopi was so tired, she thought she was hallucinating when the man appeared across the mist rising off the pool. The spa area wasn't yet open, and the locks were on a timer. The only means of entry was the use of a staff card, and she was the employee on shift. The man's robe wasn't hotel issue, either, but that wasn't too unusual. Frequent guests often brought their own robes so it was easier to track where they'd left them. Even so, she'd never seen anyone show up in anything like that gorgeous crimson with gold trim and embroidered initials.

As she squinted her tired eyes at the man's stern profile and closely trimmed beard, she recognized—

Oh God. He was completely naked under that robe!

She should have looked away but didn't. *Couldn't.*

Through the steam rising off the pool, she watched him unbelt and open his robe, drop it off his shoulders to catch on his bent arms. The muscled globes of his bare butt appeared as he turned and slid free of the robe, draping it over the glass half wall that formed the rail around the pool. He was sculpted like an Olympic swimmer with broad shoulders, narrow hips and muscular thighs.

He pivoted back to face her across the pool, utterly, completely, gloriously naked. A shadow of hair accented the intriguing contours that sectioned his chest and abdomen, streaking out to dark nipples and arrowing down his eight-pack abs to—

He dived into the water, shallow and knife sharp, barely making a ripple.

She pushed her face into the stack of towels she held, no longer breathing as she tried to suppress her shock and abject mortification. She fought to push back a rising blush of hot embarrassment and something she didn't even recognize.

Because she had not only seen their special guest, the prince of Verina, in a private moment. She'd seen the crown jewels.

And of *course* she was standing on the far side of the pool where the spare caddy of clean towels was tucked beneath an overhang, next to the bar that operated in the summer months.

To escape, she would have to circle the deck, walk over the little bridge that separated the main pool from the portion that jutted out from the cliff and move past the robe he'd thrown over the rail near the glass doors into the building.

There was a small splash of water breaking as he surfaced near her feet.

"Good morning." His voice was surprised and carried the gravel of early morning.

Oh *God.* She made herself lift her face and briefly—very briefly—glanced his way.

Okay. Only his head and shoulders were visible. That ought to have made breathing possible, but dear Lord, he was good-looking. His cheekbones were carved marble above his sleek beard. Was he deliberately using the short, dark stubble to accentuate how beautiful his mouth was? Because it framed lips that managed to be both well defined and masculine, swirling wicked thoughts into her mind just looking at them. His hair was slicked back, his eyes laser blue and lazily curious.

"En français?" he tried.

"What? I mean, pardon? I mean, no. I speak English. Good morning," she managed *very* belatedly and clumsily.

At least he didn't know who she was. She had put on her one decent dress last night, planning to form part of the greeting party with Maude and her stepsisters. A last-minute mix-up with a delivery had had her changing into jeans and boots to drive two hours each way so she could fetch high-grade coffee beans and other groceries that Maude had ordered specifically for the prince's menu.

"I'm restocking towels." Not staring or tongue-tied or anything. She hurried to shove the stack into the caddy, snatching one back. "I'll leave this one with your robe. Our… um… European hour is actually…um…ten o'clock. At *night*."

"Euro…? Oh." The corner of his mouth dug in on one side. "Am I supposed to wear a swimsuit?"

"Most of our guests do." All of them. "Aside from the few who prefer to sauna au naturel. At *night*," she repeated.

"The sun hasn't come up. Technically, it's still night." He lifted a dark winged brow at the gleam of bright steel along the seam where pearly peaks met charcoal sky.

"Point taken." She drummed her fingers against her thigh, debated a moment, then decided to tease him right back. "But technically the pool isn't open yet. You're breaking our rules either way."

"What's the penalty? Because I don't expect anyone here packed a bikini top. Only a few will bother with bottoms. We don't wear them at the health spas at home. I expect that's where your 'European hour' label came from."

Pressed against the wall of the pool, he looked exactly like every other guest who might fold his arms against the edge and gaze at the view or strike up a friendly conversation with passing staff.

Except she knew he was naked, and his banter was flipping her heart and fanning the nervous excitement in her stomach. She hugged the single towel to her middle, trying to still those butterflies.

"At least I understand why Maude didn't want children running around this week. Apparently, we're hosting a nudist convention."

He smiled, the light in his eyes so warm she curled her toes in her sandals, unable to stem the shy smile that pulled at her own lips.

"You Americans are so adorably prudish."

Oh no, he didn't. She narrowed her eyes. "And you French are so—oh, I'm sorry. Are you not French?" She batted her lashes as his good humor blanked to affront.

Since Maude's announcement that he was coming here, she'd taken the time to learn that Verina was a small kingdom in the Alps between Switzerland, Germany and France. Verinians spoke all of those countries' languages and, having overcome an uprising twenty years ago that had had their neighbors sniffing and circling, trying to extend their borders to encompass Verina for the next fifteen years, were fiercely patriotic to the flag they still flew.

"I find people from *North* America to have very conservative views about sex and nudity," he clarified.

She nodded her forgiveness of his faux pas and explained, "We're not that prudish in Canada. We keep our clothes on because we're cold." She pointed at the lazy drift of tiny flakes hitting the steam off the pool and dissolving. Strangely, she wasn't feeling the chill nearly as much as she usually would, standing out here in the predawn frost. Heat radiated from her middle. Her joints were melting and growing loose.

"You must be in this pool often, though. You've never swum naked in it?"

"Never." She couldn't recall when she had last had a chance to swim at all. She vacuumed and scoured and restocked and never enjoyed the luxury she provided to everyone else.

If I can just get Maude and the girls out of here was her mantra. If she could take control of the books and balance them, quit financing trips and clothing for women who brought no value to the spa, only drama, she could relax instead of burning out.

"It's very freeing. You should try it."

"I'm sure it is." He had no idea of the constraints she was under, though.

"No time like the present."

As she met his gaze with a rueful smile, certain he was mocking her for her modesty, something in his gaze made her heart judder to a stop in her chest then kick into a different rhythm.

He was looking at her with consideration, as though he'd suddenly noticed something about her that had snagged one hundred percent of his attention. As though he was serious about wanting her to strip naked and jump in the pool with him.

More insistent tugs and pulls accosted her midsection. A flush of sensual heat streaked up from her tense stomach, warming her chest and throat and cheeks. Her breasts grew heavy and tight.

She *never* reacted to men—not like this, all receptive and intrigued. Her last date had been in high school and ended with a wet kiss that hadn't affected her nearly as strongly as this man's steady gaze. The dating pool in Lonely Lake was very small unless she wanted to get together with guests, and she didn't do that because they didn't stick around.

That's what this is, she realized, clunking back from a brief, floaty fantasy of a prince taking an interest in a nobody like her. This wasn't *real* flirty banter. He wasn't genuinely interested in her. He was only inviting her to join him in the way male guests occasionally did because she was *here*, not because he found her particularly attractive. How could he? She looked especially hellish this morning. She was frazzled and exhausted, no makeup, clothes rumpled as though she'd slept in them. Joke was on him. She *hadn't* slept.

Maybe this wasn't even happening. Maybe she would wake after being dragged from the igloo room and defrosted from a hypothermia-induced delirium.

"I'm sure you'll have plenty of company soon enough," she said in a strangled voice. She nodded upward at the windows lighting behind curtains as guests began to stir. "I'll check the saunas. They're banked at night, but I'll make sure they're up to temperature for you."

As the owner, Sopi could have asked that he wear a towel around the resort, but she didn't want to introduce herself. She was too embarrassed at thinking, even for a second, that he might genuinely be interested in her.

Besides, if he climbed out to shake her hand, buck naked, she would die.

Rhys watched her walk away with a surprising clench of dismay, even though he knew better than to flirt with the help.

He hadn't even realized anyone had been on

the pool deck until he'd surfaced after swimming the length underwater. But there she was, face buried in a stack of towels like an ostrich, her dark hair gathered into a fraying knot, her uniform mostly shapeless except where it clung lovingly to a really nice ass.

Arrogant as he innately was, he didn't expect servants to turn their face to the wall as his father had once told him his great-grandmother had demanded of palace staff.

This young woman had obviously recognized him. Nearly every woman of any age reacted to him—which he made a habit of ignoring. His reputation as a playboy was greatly exaggerated. Affairs complicated an already complex life. When he did entangle himself, he stuck with a long-term arrangement with a sophisticated partner, one who had a busy life herself. He kept ties loose until the woman in question began to suggest marriage would improve their relationship, invariably claiming it would "give us more time together" or "draw us closer"—two assumptions he knew would prove false.

Sometimes they brought up a desire for

children, and he had had good reasons for putting that off, too. Until recently.

But until very recently, Rhys hadn't believed he'd have to marry at all. Staying single had been his greatest luxury and one of the few genuine freedoms available to him. Occasionally, he had thought a wife might be the best way to stave off the fortune hunters who constantly stalked him, but marriage and family were yet more responsibilities on top of an already heavy mantle. He had thought to indefinitely postpone both.

Besides, he didn't deserve the sort of happily-ever-after his brother was striving for.

A shrieking giggle from a balcony above had him glancing up to see a pair of women in negligees exhibiting all the excitement of children spotting a monkey at the zoo. Their bare legs and cleavage flashed as they posed against the rail and waved.

And so it starts, he thought tiredly.

He looked for the young woman who had seemed so charmingly real, planning to ask her to lock out the masses for another thirty minutes.

He couldn't see her, and his irritation ratcheted up several notches. It had little to do with the looming interruption of his peaceful swim. She was gone, and he was uncomfortable with how annoyed that made him. He hadn't even asked her name.

She worked here, he reminded himself. He would see her again, but the knowledge did nothing to ease his impatience.

He shouldn't *want* to see her again. He wouldn't be able to approach her when he did. A guest coming on to an employee was a hard limit. There was an entire hotel brimming with beautiful, available, *appropriate* women if he wanted to get laid.

His nether regions weren't twitching for the silk-draped knockouts hurrying to throw on robes and rush down here, though. He was recollecting a face clean of makeup and eyes like melted chocolate framed in thick lashes. She'd had a tiny beauty spot below one corner of her mouth and what had looked like a man's wedding band on a thin chain in the hollow of her throat. Whose? A father, he imagined. She was too young to be a widow.

She could be married, though. She was very pretty, neither voluptuous nor catwalk slender, but pert with small, firm breasts, narrow shoulders and that valentine of a derriere. He had wondered how tall she would be if he stood beside her. He might get a crick in his neck when he leaned down to taste her pillowy lips—

No.

With a muttered curse, he caught his breath and dived to the bottom of the pool, using the pressure and exertion to work out his animal urges.

It didn't work. She stayed on his mind all day.

Sopi remained emotionally wired until she heard the prince had left the building. She watched the helicopter veer across the valley, climb above the tree line and wheel to the far side of a peak.

Deflated and depleted, she slipped away to her cabin for a nap. Of the half dozen tiny A-frame guest cottages, this one was farthest from the main building. At some point, probably when the stove conked out, it had become a storage unit for spare mattresses and mini refrigerators. Sopi kept one plugged in for her own use, and the heat still worked, so it was quite livable.

The tiny loft above the storage area was hardly on a par with the rest of the accommodation at Cassiopeia's, though. Even the employees had proper flats in the staff lodge tucked into the trees. That building was boxy and utilitarian, but they each had their own bedroom, bathroom and kitchenette. It was well tended and cozy.

Until her father had died very suddenly when she was fifteen, Sopi had lived in the manager's suite across from the kitchen. Somehow that had been given to the manager Maude had hired to run the spa that first year. Maude had taken over the suite when she came back to run things herself, except her version of managing was to delegate everything to Sopi.

Sopi had meanwhile bounced through guest and staff units as they became available. Eventually, she had wound up on the fringe of the property while Maude's daughters had appropriated the top suite when they returned to complain about having to live here instead of gadding about Europe.

Sopi didn't love tramping through the snow in the dark, but she did love having her own space. She had managed to warm it up with a few cherished items of her mother's—a blue velvet reading chair and a faded silk area rug. Her bed, purchased from the buy-and-sell ads, was a child's bunk bed with a desk beneath. Cartoon princesses adorned it, but they inspired her to dream, so she hadn't painted over them.

A long time ago, a guest had started the silly rumor that the owner of this hotel was descended from royalty. He had thought Sopi's mother had been the daughter of an ousted king or something.

Sopi's mother had already been gone by that point. Her father had only chuckled and shaken his head. It was a nice legend that might bring curiosity seekers to the spa, he'd said, but nothing more.

Sopi sighed and climbed into her bed without eating. The stacked milk crates that formed her pantry were empty. She hadn't had time to buy a box of cereal or replenish the instant soup she kept on hand to make with the kettle that was her most reliable friend.

Her head hit the pillow, and she plunged into a sleep so deep she wouldn't have heard a bomb go off.

Yet when the distant rat-a-tat of helicopter blades began to sound in the distance, her eyes snapped open.

Dang. She'd been dreaming something sexy about hot pool waters sliding silkily across her skin while a pair of blue eyes—

Ugh. She was so pathetic.

And wide-awake now that a mixture of self-contempt and guilt had hold of her. She glanced at her phone. It was full of text messages from staff. Some made her laugh. They all got on really well, but it was work, too. She had a quick shower, dressed and hurried back.

After putting out three proverbial fires, she was in the mani-pedi salon listening to a nail technician complain about an order of decals shaped like high-heeled shoes.

"They were supposed to be more bedazzled, but instead they're this plain black, and when you put clear polish on them, they curl up and fall off."

Sopi frowned and took the polish and decals to a bench at the back of the salon. All the mani-pedi chairs were full of buzzing women hoping to meet the prince later.

From the time she was twelve, Sopi had apprenticed in all the treatments under a multitude of formally trained staff. She didn't have any certificates on the wall, but she could pinch-hit with nearly any service from foiled streaks to Swedish massage. If there'd been a chair free, she would have pitched in to help with the roster of guests begging for polish, but she had too much to do elsewhere anyway.

At least she'd taken the time last week to give her own toenails a fresh, if unremarkable, coat of pale pink polish. She stuck the decals of high-heeled shoes on each of her big toes and shellacked them in place with clear polish. She bedazzled one with a couple of glinting sequins to see if that would help hold it in place and make it look prettier.

She was curled over, blowing on her toes, distantly listening to a pair of women speculate on what time the prince would appear for dinner and whether he would invite anyone to join his table, when she picked up a call that had her frowning and hurrying barefoot down the hall to the massage therapy rooms.

Karl, their beefy Norwegian masseur, wasn't on the schedule this week, but Sopi spotted him about to enter a closed door.

"Karl!" she whispered. They strongly discouraged any conversation above a whisper in the spa area to ensure the guests enjoyed a relaxing stay. "It's your wife." She offered her phone.

Face blanking with panicked excitement, Karl took the phone and spoke rapidly in Norwegian.

"I have to go," he said, ending the call and trying to pocket Sopi's phone. "The midwife is on her way. It's time."

"Finally! Hurry home, then." Sopi couldn't help grinning as she stole back her phone. "I hope everything goes well."

"Thank you." He started away, turned back, clearly in a flummoxed state of mind. "My phone is still in there. He's on the table!"

"Karl." Sopi took his arm and spoke calmly

and firmly. "Don't worry about your client. I'll cover your massage. Get your phone and go home to your wife."

He nodded, knocked gently and led Sopi into the room.

"Sir, I'm very sorry," he said as he entered. "My wife has gone into labor, but I'm leaving you in good hands. Literally. Ah, there it is." Karl retrieved his phone from the small shelf above the essential oils. He turned to Sopi. "And she did text me, but I missed it because I silence it out of habit when I'm consulting with a client. The prince felt a twist in his lower back while skiing. He wants to be sure it doesn't turn into anything serious."

Sopi nodded dumbly, throat jammed as she avoided staring at the muscled back on the massage table, a sheet draped loosely across his hips and legs.

"Thank you," Karl said to her as he hurried from the room.

Sopi drew a breath and choked on a speck of spit. She turned her cough into a cleared throat, managing to croak, "I apologize for the switch. Karl was on call this week. I don't think he would have come in for anyone else but you."

The prince's shoulders tensed as though the sound of her voice surprised him.

She moved to tug the sheet over his exposed foot and straightened the rest of it as she moved up the far side of the table. When she started to tuck the edge of the sheet under the band of his underwear, she realized he wasn't wearing any. Big hairy surprise. How was this her life?

CHAPTER TWO

"I'M NOT FORMALLY TRAINED, but I've apprenticed under all of our registered therapists. I have over four hundred hours of treatments."

It was her. She had a touch as light as her footsteps moving quietly around the table. The room held a vague scent of citrus and sage, but he detected a scent beneath it. The sharp bite of nail polish and something more subtle, like sun-warmed peaches.

"Is your injury serious enough I should arrange a doctor or physiotherapist to come in? I don't want to exacerbate anything."

"You can't hurt me." He nearly laughed at the idea, but there was already an uncomfortable compression in his groin that might become a serious ache if he didn't keep a firm grip on his straying thoughts. "I typically ask for a man because women usually aren't aggressive enough. It's only a small twinge. I should have warmed up properly with my swim this morning, but the pool became too busy for laps." Too busy, period. He'd left when the first women arrived and had had to swim up a stream of crestfallen faces on his way to the elevator.

She set a hand on the back of his calf and squeezed, then moved it down to his ankle and squeezed again. It was a silent communication to let him know where she was, but it was surprisingly firm. Confident.

"I'll use our unscented oil. If there's significant inflammation, I can add geranium or yarrow."

He almost suggested she could dress him like a salad, but bit it back. He didn't usually have to filter himself quite so carefully when he was alone with a woman. He was the one naked and facedown, pretty much at her mercy, but an urge to pursue gripped him. He had to be careful.

"Whatever you think is best."

"How was the snow?" She was on his left side.

"Good." Amazing, actually. The sun had come out and the powder had been chest deep, but he barely recalled it now as he heard the click of a cap and the quiet friction of her palms rubbing together. He discovered he was holding his breath with anticipation.

Her fingertips settled in his middle back, light as a leaf coming to rest on the ground. Slowly, she applied pressure until she was leaning into him, prompting him to exhale until there was nothing left in his lungs.

As he drew in his next breath, the warmth in her hands stayed firm, penetrating his skin. She began to move in sweeping strokes, spreading the oil before her touch slowed and grew more exploratory.

Rhys had a massage at least once a month. He was as athletic as possible given his busy life of travel and meetings. He worked out regularly and ran marathons on treadmills, but he had a knack for storing tension in his shoulders and neck.

She found it, squeezing his trapezius muscle on either side, not working it, but acknowledging it. It wasn't supposed to be erotic, but he found her greeting of that tension both teasing and soothing. A comforting warning that she would be back.

It fostered a sense of connection that he instinctively knew would make for both heaven and hell. He probably should have called this massage off right here and now, but the temptation to feel her hands on him was too strong. Even though he doubted he'd be able to relax when—

He grunted with shock as she set her thumb into a spot next to his spine and sent a white-hot blade between his ribs.

"Sorry." Her touch lifted away. "Trigger point. I'll come back to it."

"No." It was as if she'd found something in him no one else had ever discovered. "Do it again."

"I just felt all this tightness here." Her hand got into the crook of his neck and shoulder while she pressed into the trigger point again with the point of—

"Is that your *elbow*?"

"Too hard?" She lifted away.

"No."

The pressure came back, the pain intense for the space of three breaths before it faded into a release of tingles like fairy dust, so profound he groaned in relief.

"There we go," she murmured, hands

sweeping to soothe before she moved to the other side.

For the next ten minutes, she worked his shoulders, alternately persecuting and appeasing before she moved into his lower back. She even nudged aside the sheet to get her elbows into the tops of his glutes. It was another pressure point, hurting like hell before the cords in his lower back relaxed and his muscles turned to pudding.

He had never considered himself kinky, but this was bordering on erotic. The whole time he was blinded by intense sensations, he was equally aware of the sensual brush of her breast against his hip and what might have been the tickle of her hair falling against his spine. When he lifted his hips slightly, trying to give himself room to grow, she straightened away and drew the sheet up over his tailbone.

"I'll try going after that area with reflexology." She uncovered his feet. "Tell me if this pressure is too much?"

Her thumbs dug against his instep. He nearly levitated, but the endorphin rush was worth it. By the time she'd gone up his calves and into his hamstrings, he was hers. He'd never been in such a state of sublime arousal. She could have tied him to the bed and shown him a riding crop and he'd have begged, "Yes, please."

She worked his arms, and it took everything in him to keep them lax rather than flexing to drag her close. He ached to touch her as intimately as she was touching him, but he had to stay motionless and let her drive him mad.

This was torture. Genuine torture.

"Would you like to turn ov—"

"No," he growled. He was fully hard. If she looked him in the eye, she would know how badly he wanted to drag her atop him and see how much abuse this table could take.

A surprised pause. "I'll finish with your neck and scalp, then?"

"Yes."

She moved to stand above his head. All he could see through the face cradle was her bare feet.

Each of her big toes wore a silhouette of a woman's shoe against a background of pink. The plain one was peeling up. The other was bedecked with jewels and winked at him as she curled her toes and set gentle fingertips against the back of his neck.

"If I've been too rough—"

"You haven't." He closed his eyes in pleasure-pain. "This is the best massage of my life. I have to cut it short before it turns into something else."

He thought he heard a small *"Eep."* He definitely heard her swallow.

"Stay mean," he growled.

Her laugh was garbled and semihysterical, but she obeyed. She did cruel things to his trapezius muscles, turning snarling pit bulls into docile golden retrievers.

The final act was a merciless grip of all four fingertips of both hands into the muscles at the base of his skull. She held him in a dull headache for what felt like ten minutes before the pain evaporated into a sensation of sunshine dawning after a long, harsh winter.

She speared her fingers into his hair and erased his memory of pain, leaving the tranquil buzz he'd only previously experienced postcoitally.

"Take your time rising and dressing." Her

voice sounded throaty and laden with desire, causing a fresh rush of heat into his groin. "Drink some water."

He couldn't move. Wait. He picked up his head, but the door was already closing behind her.

He felt drugged as he sat up, peeved that he hadn't asked her name. Probably for the best. He looked down at his lap, as ready for sex as he'd ever been.

If she could put him through his paces with a massage, what would sex with her be like?

The strong tug between his thighs told him thoughts like that were unhelpful.

As he pulled on his robe, he resented the hell out of his position. Curse tradition and snobbery and an illness that had put the future on his doorstep. Ten years ago, he could have had an affair with a spa worker and no one would have known or cared.

Once he'd moved back into the palace, he'd had to become more circumspect in his choices, but he still could have managed a fling with someone whose connections were less prestigious than his own. There would have been blowback, but an affair wasn't marriage.

That's what Rhys had to court now, though. Any relationship he started would have to be taken to the finish line. Was he really going to go against the grain with a pool-girl masseuse? Refuse to do his duty to his brother and the crown in favor of appeasing his libido?

He cursed, annoyed. One dinner was all he was after, before he made the rounds through the more expected choices of potential brides. Was that so much to ask? One evening to get to know her before he was forced to settle?

It was a selfish rationalization he shouldn't even contemplate.

He poured a cup of water from the cistern and threw it back like a shot of scotch. As he kicked into his sandals by the door, he almost mistook the speck on the tiles for a spider, but no.

He bent and touched his fingertip to it, picking up the silhouette of a woman's shoe, just like the one that had been coming off her toe. Huh.

Pinching it between his finger and thumb, he tucked it deep into the pocket of his robe, considering.

Flushed and confused, Sopi hurried to get as far away from the prince as possible, all the way to the other end of the building, where the service entrance to the kitchen was located. She stood on the back stoop in the cold dusk, trying to bring herself back under control.

She had provided a lot of massages, usually to women, but many to men, and had never once felt so affected by the experience. It hadn't been lascivious, either. It had been... elemental. She'd never become so entranced by a deep and genuine yearning to ease and soothe and heal. Yet touching him had been stimulating, too, keeping her in a state of alert readiness. Like petting a giant cat.

Or a man in peak condition who appealed to her on a primitive level.

She could have stroked her hands over him for hours, like a sculptor lovingly sanding her creation to a fine polish. In those last seconds before she'd asked him to roll over, she had felt a strong urge to splay herself atop him. Blanket him with her body while soaking in his essence.

Truthfully, she'd been lost in her world at that point and had been shocked back to reality when he declined to turn faceup.

I have to cut it short before it turns into something else.

She'd been stunned. Embarrassed that she'd aroused him, but shaken and inflamed by the idea. All the banked sexual energy she'd been suppressing as she administered the massage had suddenly engulfed her in a rush of carnal hunger.

If he hadn't told her to "stay mean," she didn't know what she might have done, but she'd found the concrete knots at the base of his skull. *Heavy is the crown*, she'd thought, wondering what his life was like back in Verina.

She would never know.

A sudden shiver had her realizing she had cooled past comfortable. She went inside, where the kitchen staff was scrambling to prepare for the dinner rush.

Without being asked, she slipped into the

change room and put on her prep cook garb, then spent an hour peeling potatoes and scrubbing pots.

She was at her sweaty, sticky worst when she headed back to her cabin for a shower. The sound of squabbling as she approached through the trees almost had her turning back.

"Sopi!" Fernanda said when she spotted her. "Where have you been? I've been texting you."

"Oh?" Sopi pretended to scan her phone.

"She blocks us, you stooge," Nanette said pithily.

"Only when I'm working," Sopi said sweetly as she slid between the two towering beauties to unlock her door. "The paying guests are my priority, seeing as they support us." Hint, hint.

"Well, this has to do with the prince, so you ought to have been paying attention." As she entered uninvited, Fernanda wrinkled her nose at the clutter.

"She wants to make a fool of herself and wants you to help," Nanette informed Sopi with an eye roll.

"Why are you here?" Fernanda charged.
"The same reason."

"To shower with me?" Sopi asked facetiously. "I don't usually entertain there."

"Shocker," Nanette muttered with an examination of her nails.

Always a joy spending time with family. Sopi bit back a sigh.

"The dining room could use you both to hostess this evening," Sopi said, mainly to Nanette. She never lifted a finger unless Maude pressed her. "We have a full house. Tables will turn over three or four times at least."

"Unavailable. Sorry," Nanette said with a saccharine smile.

"Not even for the chance to seat the prince?"

"He's not eating downstairs," Fernanda jumped in to say. "That's why I'm here. Women are lined up out the door at the salon to get one of these." Fernanda handed Sopi a sheet of toe decals.

Sopi frowned. "They're defective. I was in the salon earlier. They fall off."

"Yes, I know that. That's why *you* have to put it on. To make sure it stays."

Sopi shook her head, almost thinking there was a compliment in there, but definitely a backhanded one.

"If you're not going to help in the dining room, I have to shower and hurry back. Stick it on yourself. It's not rocket science."

"Forget the dining room," Fernanda said with a stamp of her foot. "No one will even show up there. The prince is dining privately. With a woman who has one of these stuck to her toe."

"What?" When she had pushed her feet into her closed-toe kitchen clogs, Sopi had noticed that she'd lost her plain shoe decal during the massage. She had only managed to keep the bedazzled one. She removed her snow boots now but self-consciously kept her socks on.

Nanette straightened from leaning against the decommissioned stove, wiping her hands across her backside as she did. "It seems the prince met someone who interests him, but he doesn't know her name. His assistant put the word out that this woman only has one shoe." She flipped her hair. "Apparently, she knows who she is, and he wants her to come to his suite this evening if she would like to dine with him."

"He—that's silly," Sopi said, hyperaware of the hot blush that flooded into her cheeks. It was a tremendous long shot that he could be talking about her. "Fernanda, he's going to know right away whether you're the woman he is trying to meet. If you don't already have a decal, you're not her."

"Well, his bodyguard doesn't know that, does he? If I can get in to see him, the prince can decide if I'm the right woman or not."

Sopi opened her mouth but couldn't find words. Fernanda wasn't the brightest candle on the cake and tended to be very self-involved. She came across as selfish, but she wasn't mean, just firmly stuck between thoughtless and clueless.

"I tried to tell her." Nanette grew more alert, like a jackal that scented something on the air. She was definitely the brains in the family, calculating and sharp.

"Yet here you are. Wanting the *same thing*," Fernanda hissed at her sister. "So it's not such a stupid idea, is it?"

"Wait." Sopi held up a hand. "Did you say there's some sort of run on at the salon?"

"Yes! Everyone is trying to get one. The girls tried to tell me to come back later, but there's no time. Can you just…" Fernanda unzipped her knee-high spiked-heel boot and dragged off her sock. "Hurry." She wiggled her toes. "I need to dress."

"Fernanda—" Sopi looked to Nanette for backup, but Nanette was also removing her ankle-high snakeskin boot. "I don't even have polish—oh."

Fernanda had absconded with a handful of bottles from the salon. Nanette had brought a tiny tube of fast acting superadhesive. She handed that over with a pointed look. *She* wouldn't lose her decal, come hell or high water.

"You're going to parade to his suite with everyone else, all wearing one shoe so he can see you have a decal on your toe?" Sopi asked with bemusement.

"I'll wear proper open-toed evening shoes, won't I? Honestly, Sopi." Fernanda rolled her eyes.

Right. Sopi was the one being ridiculous.

Since it was the fastest way to get these two women to leave her private space, Sopi sat on the stairs to her loft. She motioned for Fernanda to set her foot beside her thigh.

"I put a pair of these on earlier," Sopi mused as she very carefully placed the shoe on Fernanda's toe. "I guess I should dress up and come with you. Maybe it's me he's looking for." It was a deliberate effort to provoke a reaction, so she shouldn't have been stung by Fernanda's dismissive snort.

"Oh, right. Have you even spoken to him for one second?"

"I have, actually." Sopi was always annoyed when these two put on that tone that disparaged her as a backwoods hick who lacked their refinement.

"What did you talk about?" Nanette asked, gaze narrowed.

"Nothing much." She shook the bottle of polish. "He didn't even ask my name." It was another dig.

She swiped the brush across the decal, varnishing the shoe into place. When she looked up, Fernanda was scowling with suspicion.

"Have you given any thought to how you'll

walk back with wet polish on your toe?" Sopi asked.

"That's why I brought the glue," Nanette said, nudging her sister aside and eyeing Sopi shrewdly. "What would you wear?" she asked.

"Hmm?" Sopi glanced up from trying to break the seal on the glue nozzle.

"To dine with the prince."

"Oh." She hadn't given one iota of thought to actually doing it, but she'd come this far into needling them. She let bravado take her a few more steps. "I have some things of my mother's. There's a vintage Chanel I've always wanted an excuse to wear."

"How am I only hearing about this now? Show me." Nanette sounded genuinely impressed, but maybe Sopi was that desperate to finally take her by surprise.

She finished gluing the shoe to Nanette's toe, then trotted up the stairs to her loft.

In the chest beneath the window, she kept a handful of keepsakes—her parents' wedding album, the Christmas ornaments that hadn't broken over the years and her audition tape to a televised singing contest that might have been her big break if her father hadn't passed away the week she was supposed to appear.

Moving all of that aside, she drew out a zipped fabric box that also stored her summer wear. She dumped her clothes onto the floor and drew out the tissue-wrapped dress.

Sopi bit her lip as she noticed the moths had been into it. Voraciously.

Nanette arrived at the top of the stairs and said, "Oh my *God*. I thought *I* lived in a hovel."

"Don't you *dare*," Sopi said, voice sharpened by the strike of painful knowledge that she had lost a prized possession. This rag only proved she was nowhere near the prince's league. "You live here for *free*. Who do you think *pays* for that?"

"You just said it. It's free. No one is making you live like this. You're the one who plays the martyr all the time. 'Oh, woe. If you don't play hostess, I have to.'"

"'Oh, woe,'" Sopi shot back. "'I can't put a sticker on my own toe.'"

"Exactly," Nanette said with a hair flip and a complete absence of apology. "Set standards for yourself and refuse to compromise them." Her scathing glance dismissed Sopi's handful of possessions and the dress that was definitely not living up to her claims.

Such a cow. If Sopi was the cretin they thought, she would push Nanette down the stairs, taking out Fernanda, who had come up behind her to make a face of amused disgust as she looked around. God, she hated both of them.

"Oh, Sopi, no," Fernanda said when she saw the dress. Her tone held the depth of sympathy one saved for muddy dogs found starving in ditches. "You have to store vintage pieces properly. Otherwise they fall apart when you wear them. Everyone knows that. What a shame."

"Clearly your standards aren't being met here," Sopi said through her teeth. "Kindly leave my hovel and never come back."

"Does this mean you won't do my hair?"

"Seriously, Fernanda?" Sopi glared.

"You don't have to be so sensitive! I don't understand why she treats us like this," Fernanda complained as the two women went down the stairs.

They left, and Sopi hurried to lock the door

so they couldn't return. Then she went into the shower and wept over old dresses and lost parents and foolish fantasies about unattainable men.

When she turned off the water, she stared at the bedazzled shoe on her one toe. Stupid. She picked it off so her nail was an ugly, chipped mess, and she left it that way as a reminder to stay grounded.

Then she wished even harder that the prince would marry one of her stepsisters and get them all out of her life for good.

"Say that again," Rhys growled at his assistant.

Gerard shifted uncomfortably. "I did as you asked. I put the word out that you were trying to locate the woman with the little shoe on her toe."

"You said I had met her already? That I knew who I was looking for?"

"Perhaps I wasn't clear on that?" His assistant's shoulders hunched up to his ears. "It seemed self-explanatory, but..." He trailed off, miserable.

"And now there's...how many women in the hall?"

"Fifty? Sixty?"

"All with one shoe on her toe."

"I'm afraid so, sir." Gerard swallowed.

"What am I supposed to do? Walk the line as though inspecting the troops, looking for her among them?" He'd been trying to be discreet. Rather than make it clear he was looking for someone on staff, he had thought he would get word to her through the grapevine. She could then quietly appear in his room if she was interested.

"How did they even get up here in the elevator?"

"The one shoe, sir. The bodyguards—"

Rhys pinched the bridge of his nose. "Suggestions on how to get rid of them?"

"Perhaps if you simply ate in the dining room? Mingled? Gave them a chance to say hello?"

Rhys had no appetite. "That never works. It only encourages them to approach me later." But he had to find himself a wife, and what was he going to do? Put a staff member in the unnerving position of having to walk a gauntlet to reach him for a single date that would go nowhere?

If she was out there and wanted to see him, she would already have knocked on his door. No, she was either too self-conscious or wasn't interested.

What a galling thought. Deep down, however, he knew it was for the best.

It still infuriated him.

"Fine," he growled. "Tell them I'll dine downstairs after all."

When the news came that the prince would in fact need a table, Sopi experienced a rush of panic. She definitely, positively didn't want to see him. After brooding for a solid hour, she had decided that what he must have meant when he cut short her massage was that he thought *she* was turning it into something it wasn't.

Unsurprisingly, her stepsisters both appeared within minutes of the announcement, eager to marshal rivals to terrible tables and have an excuse to brush past the prince's table while he ate. He would sit with the handful of upper-crust bachelors who had accompanied him onto the slopes and were providing further red meat for the marriage-minded women hungry for a good match.

Sopi gladly relinquished the reservation desk and slipped into the laundry room to help fold sheets and towels.

With nearly every guest now rubbing elbows in the dining room, the rest of the building was quiet. She stuck with her friends in housekeeping, joking and exchanging light gossip about the guests as they restocked the linen cupboards and performed the turndown service in the top-floor rooms.

She did the prince's room herself and, as she plumped the pillow, noticed the tiny black shoe on the night table. It sat atop one of the burgundy portfolios Maude liked to use for special event meetings. She would make a note from a bride or other VIP guest, then snap it shut and hand it off to Sopi with instructions to make things happen.

Sopi's pulse tripped at the sight of the tiny shoe, but a bodyguard stood by observing her, so she closed the drapes, set wrapped chocolates on the pillow and left.

Eventually, the guests retired from the dining room to hit the hot pools. Most of them were drunk and she resigned herself to a lot of cleanup later but helped the kitchen recover first.

While she was there, Maude pulled her aside with another list of to-dos. By the time they were done, it was time to close the pool and saunas. As Sopi marshaled the stragglers out, fully eight people tried to bribe her into calling them if the prince showed up after hours.

She bundled the last naked nymph into a robe and onto an elevator, then switched everything to service. That locked off the treatment level to all but the staff cards. She sighed in relief, facing miles to go before she slept, but the closing chores were ones she almost enjoyed. She could do them at her own pace and no one ever interrupted her.

Humming, she wheeled the mop from the closet and got started.

Midnight and Rhys was wide-awake, standing at the window, wired.

Wondering.

Swearing at himself. At his brother. At life.

For two hours, he'd been surrounded by beautiful, eligible, well-bred women, none of whom had been the one he wanted to see. It wasn't like him to be so fixated. He didn't like it. He'd seen the dark side of humans who became obsessed.

The darkest night of his life replayed un-invited. His well-practiced ability to block it didn't work this time, and his head filled with the shouts and crashing and what he'd thought had been fireworks inside the palace.

He'd been ten, old enough to take in the full horror of being invaded by soldiers in military garb and the gravity of their holding his parents at gunpoint below. He'd been too young to make a difference, though. In fact, he'd made things worse. He had screamed and rushed to the top of the stairs, where Henrik was being held off by a soldier.

If he had halted beside Henrik, his parents might still be alive. He had gone for the soldier's gun, though, and the soldier had crashed him in the face with the butt of his rifle, splitting his cheek and knocking him onto his ass.

Rhys had heard his mother scream. She had

started to race up the stairs to him. A soldier below grabbed her arm and yanked her back. His father intervened, and the tension below erupted into four shots that left his parents crumpled on the floor.

Rhys could still feel the unnatural strength in Henrik as he'd gripped the shoulders of Rhys's pajamas and dragged him backward, behind the half wall of the upper gallery. Rhys had been limp with shock, gaze held by the cold stare of the soldier who had shot his parents so remorselessly.

He would never forget the ugly lack of humanity in that pair of eyes. He would forever carry the weight of guilt that if he hadn't given in to his own impulses, his parents might be alive today.

Distantly, he'd been aware of Henrik stammering out pleas. Promises they would never come back if they were allowed to leave. He'd somehow got Rhys onto his feet and pulled him down the service stairs and out of the palace.

Shock had set in and Rhys didn't recall much of the days after that, but guilt remained a heavy cloak on him. Guilt and loss and failure. He was grateful to Henrik for getting them out, but a day never went by where he didn't feel sick for escaping. For surviving when his parents had died because of his rash actions.

A day never went by when he didn't feel their loss as though pieces had been carved out of his heart. His chest throbbed even more acutely with apprehension over Henrik's diagnosis.

Why Henrik? It should be him staring into the muzzle of a life-threatening diagnosis, not his brother. If he lost Henrik—

He couldn't let himself think it.

This was why he hadn't wanted to marry and have children. This agonizing fear and inability to control the future were intolerable.

He swore under his breath.

If grim introspection was the only mood he could conjure, he needed a serious distraction. He walked across to the folio Maude had given him, the one he had said he wanted to review when he had made his abrupt exit from the dining room earlier this evening.

Maude's eldest daughter, a lithe beauty, had

fallen into step alongside him as he departed, offering an excuse about fetching something from her room. Her purpose had been obvious, though. She had deliberately created the impression she was the one he'd been seeking as his dinner companion. In the elevator, she had set her pretty silver shoe next to his, not quite nudging, but definitely inviting him to notice her toe.

This constant circling was exhausting. In the space of a day, he'd come around from thinking he *should* marry to impatience for task completion. Maude's eldest was exactly what was expected of the royal family— well-bred, smoothly sophisticated and picture-perfect beautiful. She struck him as the possessive type, too. Overtures from other women would no longer be a problem. She would make damned sure of it.

"Please allow me to arrange a more peaceful dining experience for you tomorrow," she had offered with the silky sweetness of a white chocolate mousse. "We often close the solarium for honeymoon couples."

Honeymoon was a deliberate choice of word, he was sure. *So* exhausting.

"I'll let you know." He had cut away to his own room, not the least bit compelled to spend another minute with her, let alone a lifetime.

As he flipped open the folio, interest in purchasing this property nonexistent, the tiny black shoe fluttered to the carpet. All the darkness in him folded in on itself, becoming a burst of light with a single focus. *Her.*

He tried to shake it off. He had no business obsessing over anyone, let alone the least suitable woman here. How did he even have the energy to experience a rush of masculine interest? He ought to be physically exhausted from his day of skiing, but he couldn't shake this buzz of sexual hunger. This sense of something being unfinished.

Maybe he could work it out in the pool.

He stripped where he stood and pulled on his robe. This time he had the sense to bring one of his bodyguards and ordered him to stand at the door to ensure he wouldn't be stalked.

The lights were dimmed in the change room, the mirror and taps polished, the floor dry. The music and water feature were both turned off, along with the jets in the tub. It was blessedly silent as he walked past the still water of the indoor pool and hot tub. Through the fogged windows, he saw steam rising off the mineral pool in gentle wafts against the black sky.

Just as he was about to walk outside and dive in, however, he heard a noise down the short hallway that led to the sauna area. A woman was singing.

The scent of eucalyptus carried with her voice on the humid air. A bucket of cleaning supplies stood outside a door to a steam room. The sound of spraying water cut off, and he clearly heard her crooning a modern ballad that reverberated beautifully off the tiled walls.

He stood transfixed as *she* emerged to drop a long-handled scrubbing brush into the bucket. Her hair was in a messy ball atop her head, but tendrils stuck to her damp neck. She wore light cotton pants and a baggy smock, both heavily soaked at the cuffs. Without looking his way, she quit singing and sighed.

She picked up the bucket and carried it down the hall and around a corner where an authorized-personnel-only sign hung.

What was she doing cleaning the sauna at midnight? She was a goddess who possessed a healing touch and a siren's voice, not a scullery maid.

He crossed his arms, scowling as he listened to a door open and close. He waited for her to reappear.

And waited.

Had she locked herself in a utility closet? He followed to the end of the hall, where he found two doors. One opened to a closet that was empty of all but fresh linens and cleaning supplies. Her bucket sat on the floor inside it.

The other door read Emergency Exit Only. Door Locks Automatically.

It hadn't set off an alarm when she went through, so he pushed it open. The night was clear, the air bracing. A narrow footpath had been stamped into the snow. He glimpsed a maintenance building in the trees.

Don't, his rational head warned.

He felt for his key card, tried it against the

mechanism on the outside and saw it turn green. He stepped into the cold and let the door lock behind him.

CHAPTER THREE

TO HELL WITH IT. That was what Sopi had been thinking the whole time she'd been scrubbing the saunas. She felt grimy and sweaty and resentful and *entitled to enjoy herself.*

Not in the treated waters of the hot pool, though. No, she was going to the source, the original spring that had been formed by long-ago explorers, possibly ancestors of the nearest First Nations tribe. No one knew exactly who had dammed the hot water trickling out of the mossy ground, forming a small bathing pool on a bluff in the woods, but through the 1800s and into the early 1900s the small swimming hole had been used by hunters and snowshoers who heard about it through word of mouth.

Eventually, an enterprising railway baron had built the first rustic hotel here. He had brought in a crew to dig a proper pool by hand, and that hole had eventually become what was the indoor pool today. He had lined it and filled it with snow that he melted and heated by piping water from this tiny hot spring. Since this natural, rocky pool was impossible to clean, the hotel wasn't allowed to let guests use it. It was kept as a heat source and a point of interest. In the summer, the gate next to the pump house was left unlocked so guests could picnic on the bench nearby, enjoying the view of the lake and the soothing trickle of the water.

Tonight, Sopi's were the only footsteps as she veered off the path to the maintenance shed and wound through the trees. The snow wasn't too deep under the laden evergreens, but she was only wearing sandals. By the time she emerged and shoved at the gate to open it against the accumulation of snow, her feet were frozen and aching.

She waded through the knee-high snow the final few yards. As she reached the edge of the pool, she kicked off her sandals and stepped into the hot water. It hurt like mad, but was a relief, too.

She hadn't been to the pool in a long time. Not since she had come out here to cry after getting the news her father had passed from a sudden heart attack. This had always been her sad place, and that moment had been one of her saddest. Since it wasn't something she liked to revisit, she didn't come here often.

She had forgotten how peaceful it was, though. The height of the trees hid it from hotel windows. The only reminders of civilization were the fence and gate and the distant hum of the pump house. She turned her back on those man-made things and faced the lake. The slope fell away, allowing a clear view of its sparkling, snow-blanketed surface.

The longer she stood here, the better she felt. The waters truly were capable of healing, she decided with a sigh of reclaimed calm. She started to pull her top up over her head but froze when she heard the crunch of footsteps.

Really? She almost screamed in frustration. Who? *Why?* She twisted to glare at—

"Oh."

"You're not supposed to swim alone." The prince's breath fogged against the frosty air. He wore his robe and rattled the gate to open it farther before he took long strides through the snow in his slippers. As he came closer, she was able to read his frown of dismay in the moonlight reflecting as a faint blue glow off the surrounding snow. He abandoned his slippers next to her sandals and stepped into the water, hissing at the bite of heat.

She looked back the way he'd come, expecting at least a few bodyguards and one or two of his cohorts, if not a full harem of adoring women.

"Are you lost? What are you doing here?" she asked him.

"What are *you* doing here?"

"You inspired me," she admitted truthfully, although Nanette's pithy talk of refusing to compromise had also lit a fire of rebellion in her.

"To try skinny-dipping? This is hotter than the pool."

"It is. Too hot in the summer, which is the only time this area is open to the public." She nodded at the sign obscured by a buildup of frozen condensation. "No swimming allowed."

"Ah. I've inspired you to break rules."

His mouth barely twitched, but he sounded pleased. "Live dangerously."

"Not really. I happen to know it's tested regularly and is always found to be potable." The fence kept wildlife out, so risk of contamination was next to zero.

"That takes some of the thrill out of it, doesn't it?"

His words made her think of her step-sisters' disparagement of her. Their contempt had gone far deeper than a scoff over a moth-eaten dress. They knew she wasn't any match for a man in his position. *Sopi* knew it. She was standing here prickly with self-consciousness, aware that she was still covered in sweat from laboring in the spa. Definitely not anywhere near his exalted level.

The water beckoned, but she murmured, "It was a dumb impulse. We should go back."

He dragged his gaze from the frozen lake, eyes glittering in the moonlight, but his expression was inscrutable. "I wanted you to join me."

"Here?" She shook her head. Part of her was tempted. Where was the harm in a nude swim with a stranger? And where had such a reckless thought come from, she wondered with a suppressed choke of laughter. But he was the first man to make her consider such rash behavior. Everything about this was a rarity for her.

"For dinner," he clarified. "Did you…get that memo?"

The air that came into her lungs seemed to crystallize to powdered ice. "I didn't imagine for a minute you were looking for me. Besides, every woman here got a decal—"

"I know that," he cut in, sounding aggravated. "Now."

She bit back a smile. "You could have sent me a proper message."

"I didn't know your name. My assistant asked the booking clerk, but Karl was listed as my masseur. Who *are* you?"

She hesitated. Tell him everything? Would he care?

"I know this is inappropriate," he growled into the silence that she let stretch out with her indecision. "That's why I didn't want to make overt inquiries."

Inappropriate? It hadn't been, not really,

until he used that word. Now she reeled, astonished that he was making this private conversation into more than she would have let herself believe it to be.

"If I'm out of line, say so. We'll go back right now."

"I don't know what this is," she admitted, hugging herself against the cold, because the hot water on her feet wasn't enough to keep her warm when she was outside at midnight before spring had properly taken hold. "My father bought this hotel for my mother. She named it after me. Cassiopeia. My friends call me Sopi."

"Cassiopeia." He seemed to taste the syllables, which made her shiver in a different way. "Maude is your mother?" He sounded surprised. Skeptical.

"Stepmother. She took control of the spa after my father died. I wasn't old enough to do it myself and... Well, I'd like to challenge her now, but lawyers cost money and... It's a long, boring story." She doubted he would believe the spa ought to belong to her anyway, not when she stood here all sweaty and gross.

"I'm really cold. Can we—" She looked for her sandals.

"Yes. Let's warm up." He skimmed off his robe, tossing it to hook on the fence before he made his way farther into the pool. Naked, of course, carefully choosing his footing on the slippery rocks.

She looked to the sky, begging for guidance from higher powers.

"It's deeper than I expected," he said with satisfaction. He sank down as he found one of the rocky ledges that had been set in place for seating. "What are you doing? You said you wanted to try this."

"Alone."

"I'll turn my head." His tone rang with *prude*.

She was wearing a bra and underwear, basically a bikini. She knew that was a rationalization to stay here and swim with a man who intrigued her, but she also liked the idea of proving she *could* interest a prince, even if she was the only one who would ever know it.

Could she?

With an internal tsk, she decided to—for once—do something for herself. She stepped out of the water long enough to drop her drawstring pants and throw off her top.

She gingerly made her way into the pool, one eye on his profile to ensure he wasn't witnessing her clumsy entry. She winced at sharp edges pressing into her soles, bent to steady herself with a hand on a submerged boulder and let out a sigh as she sank to her shoulders and heat penetrated to her bones.

The pool was about four feet deep and maybe six feet wide. The prince had found one of the best perches facing the lake. She bumped her foot into his and he looked at her.

"Cheater," he accused as he noticed her bra strap.

She ducked under, unable to resist the lure of baptizing herself even though her hair would freeze into its tangled bun. Her long, strenuous day began to rinse away as she did it again. She came up with another sigh of sheer luxury.

"I didn't bring a towel. This is literally the dumbest idea I've ever had, but I don't regret it one bit."

"I would be a gentleman and offer you my

robe, but then I'd have to streak like a bald yeti across the snow to get back inside."

"I'm pretty sure I saw one of those this morning."

His teeth flashed white. "Have you always lived here? You're Canadian?"

"I am. My mother was Swedish, I think. I don't have much information on her. She was an only child, and my father was funny about her family. Didn't like to talk about them. I don't think my grandparents approved of him."

"Why not?"

"Snobs, maybe? He sold two-way pagers and the early mobile phones into the European markets. Not very sexy at the time, but it was lucrative. That's how he paid for this." She nodded toward the hotel hidden by the spiky trees. "Then Silicon Valley crashed the party. His heart trouble started when my mother passed, and financial worries made it worse."

Sopi didn't know what kind of means Maude had pretended she had, but based on what Sopi had learned since, she believed Maude had misrepresented herself and worked on her father's desire for Sopi to have a mother with the goal of taking over his bank account and assets.

"It's a strange purchase for someone in that industry, especially since you don't have cell service beyond the hotel."

"My mother was struggling as a new mom in a new country. Dad traveled a lot, and she didn't have anyone to rely on. She wasn't working and felt very isolated. She loved her spa visits, though. She came here on one of them, talked to the owner who was thinking of selling. My father bought it for her."

"Romantic."

"Not really. It was worse for wear, and she had a lot of challenges with its remote location. She knew what she wanted, though, and made it happen. It was quite successful until she passed a few years later."

"What happened?"

"A bad flu that turned into pneumonia. Can we not talk about that? I was quite young, but it still makes me sad."

"I understand," he said gravely.

She recalled a bleak line in the history of Verina stating his parents had been killed in an uprising, forcing him and his brother to live in neighboring countries for fifteen years. For the first time, she wondered if the platitude he'd just used was actually true. Maybe he really did understand the hollow ache inside her.

He had braced his elbows on nearby rocks above the surface and tipped his head back to look up at the clear sky.

She took stock of where she was, soaking with a prince in the wilderness, the only sound a distant hum and a closer trickle of water seeping from the seams in the rocks and off a worn ledge into their bath.

"There you are." He tilted his head. "The trees were in the way. Cassiopeia."

Hardly anyone used her whole name, not when they addressed her. She'd begun to think *Cassiopeia* only applied to things that weren't really hers.

"A queen, if memory serves." It was hard to read his expression with the shadows and his beard.

She almost mentioned the silly rumor about her mother being descended from royalty but thought he might think she was trying to elevate herself to his stratosphere.

"A vain one who gets tied to a chair for eternity," she said instead. "Maybe I am vain." She didn't look for the W in the sky, having searched it out nearly every starry night since childhood. "My tiny mind was blown when I learned on the first day of school that not everyone had their own constellation."

He snorted. "I don't."

"Because you're a star on earth."

"Don't," he said flatly. The steam seemed to gust off the water so there was no mist between them, only clear, dry air that stung her cheeks and nose. "Don't put distance between us."

She swallowed her surprise, but a lump lodged in her chest, one that her voice had to strain to speak around. "There is a continent and an ocean between us." Among other things. His mountain of society and stature, her vast desert of education and life experience.

"Rhys," he said, laying down a gauntlet. "If you're going to reject me, use my name so I'm clear that you mean me." It was such an outrageously arrogant statement she wanted to laugh, yet he drew her in as his equal by offering the familiarity. Such an enigmatic man.

"I thought I was pointing out the obvious," she said quietly.

"You're the least obvious person I've ever met. Any other woman would be naked and straddled across me by now, whether I wanted her here or not. You wouldn't even come to dinner with me. Why not?"

Cowardice.

"I didn't think you were serious," she repeated. "Where would this even go? That's not opportunism talking. I don't have affairs with rich, powerful men. You tell me what happens. How long does it last? What happens when it's over?"

His eyes were obsidian, his jaw gleaming like wet iron. With a muttered curse in what sounded like German, he turned his glower toward the frozen lake below.

He didn't tell her she was wrong.

Sopi felt for another of the worn rocks that provided a rough seat and settled onto it. "Do you want the truth?"

"Always," he bit out.

"Maude wants you to marry Nanette. I thought if I facilitated that, I could get rid of all three of them and finally have my home to myself."

A pulse of astounded silence, then he barked out a humorless laugh. He snapped his head around to glare at her. "I'll marry if and whom *I* desire. It won't be either of them. I promise you that right now."

She kissed goodbye her pipe dream of being free of her stepfamily, which left her to contemplate whether she should allow herself to get closer to this compelling man who, for the moment, at least, was not that far away.

"I don't know what happens, Sopi. I wish I did," he said cryptically.

At the sound of her nickname on his lips, she found herself trying out the sound of his. "Rhys." It caught with tugging sensations in her chest and across her shoulders.

He looked at her.

Everything altered. The air shimmered and the earth stood still. Her scalp prickled and her breasts grew tight and heavy.

"That does not sound like a rejection,

süsse." His voice melted her bones. He extended a long arm across the surface of the water, palm up in invitation.

She hadn't consciously meant to turn this into anything, but her hand went into his. She floated across the short space between them, drawn by his firm grip to set her hand against his neck. The top of her foot hit a rock, and she reacted with a jerk of her knee, knocking it into his.

He made a noise of concern and gathered her into his lap. His hand cupped her knee and he soothed her kneecap with his thumb. "Tell me," he murmured. "Do you feel the same when I touch you?"

"The same as what?"

The hand behind her back ran up to cradle her neck. With the lightest squeeze, he had her shuddering and turning her torso into his.

"Like that," he growled, lips coming close enough to nibble at her chin. "The way you made me feel on the table today."

Streaks of light and heat seemed to shoot through her at the graze of his whiskers and the mere touch of his mouth on her skin. She cupped his wet beard and searched for his lips with her own, not really knowing what she was doing, only knowing she needed the press of his mouth to her own.

They both moaned as their lips parted and slid and found the right fit. Forever, she thought. She wanted the forceful play of his mouth to consume hers forever. Then his tongue touched her inner lip, delved, and the taste of him shot lightning through her again, spearing a jolt of pleasure straight between her thighs.

She jerked away to catch her breath, stunned, but went straight back after his mouth, pressing the back of his head to encourage him to ravage her.

He growled and they kissed with more fervor, wildly, deeply, a sound rumbling in his chest like a predatory animal. His arms flexed around her, drawing her tighter into his lap and twisting her chest to rub against his.

Her bra shifted as they slithered against one another, abrading and annoying her as it kept her from feeling him with all her skin. She tried to scrabble behind herself with one hand and release it, but his confident fingers met hers and easily unclasped it. She drew back to pull her arms free and he threw it into the snow.

As she pressed herself into him, their mouths crashed together again. His hand swirled a rush of water across her ribs right before his palm flattened against her skin, stroked and shifted, teasing at her waist and shoulder blade and back to her rib cage until she couldn't stand it. She twisted, offering her breast, and finally he claimed the swell in a firm clasp. He shaped and caressed and made her forget everything but the feel of him fondling her so blatantly.

She realized a keening noise was coming from her lips and tried to bite it back, but he caught her nipple in a light pinch and once again she had to break from their kiss to catch her breath—the sensation was so sharp.

"Too much?" He bowed his head over hers as she buried her face in his neck, as though shielding her from something. "You're killing me."

She realized that wasn't just her own heart slamming unsteadily against her rib cage. His was, too. And that hard shape against her hip was him, fully aroused.

She stilled, shocked and stunned and wickedly curious.

"I don't have a condom," he muttered. "This is definitely the best and worst idea you've ever had." He found her ear and flicked his tongue along the rim, making her shudder. "Are you on anything? Should we take this upstairs?"

Dazzled, it took her a moment to realize what he was asking. "I'm not on anything. I don't do this. I've never done it."

"I'm not a guest. You're not an employee. Not right now. That's not what this is. It's two people who can't keep their hands off each other." He cursed and shifted her, but the sound he made was more a groan of suffering. He sucked on her lobe so hard she nearly came out of her skin. Then he applied his teeth, just short of pain, holding her in a tingling state between fear and trust.

If she pulled away, it would hurt, but she didn't want to go anywhere. She petted her fingers across his wet beard, soothing the beast who held her in his tense jaws. Her pulse throbbed in her throat and low in that secretive place between her clamped thighs.

"I mean I've *never* done this," she admitted in a quavering voice. "Made love. With anyone."

His arms nearly squashed her breathless, and a strangled noise came out of him.

"Are you serious?" He took hold of her wet, knotted hair, holding her so her nose was nearly touching his. His eyes were depthless black orbs, threatening to pull her into another universe. Her heart galloped so hard, she thought her chest would explode.

"Who would I sleep with? No one has ever made me feel like this."

"How?" His hand tightened in her hair, pulling her head back to expose her throat. He licked along the artery, and her nipples contracted to such tight points, they felt pierced. She pinched her thighs together.

"Like I'm on fire," she gasped. "Like I need your hands all over me to put it out."

His ragged laugh rang with satisfaction. This time when he claimed her breast, she arched into his touch. He caught her nipple in the crook of two fingers and applied tender pressure until she set her open teeth against his neck.

His caress was so delicious, she found herself sucking the skin of his neck against her teeth before she realized what she was doing and pulled back.

"Mark me, *süsse*." He gentled his touch and circled his thumb around her turgid, stimulated nipple, soothing. "Don't be scared. I won't hurt you. But I do want this." His arms hardened as he lifted her.

Her shoulders and chest came out of the water. As the cold hit her and tightened her nipples even more, he closed his mouth over one. The sudden shifts in temperature and his hard pull sent a jolt of electricity through her. She squeaked and clenched her hand in his hair.

He made a noise of sympathy and drew back to blow and lick circles around her nipple, making her sob under a fresh onslaught of blinding sensation.

She didn't know what to do. Wires of tension pulled in her abdomen and lower. It was more than she could take, but she was greedy, too. She folded her arms around the back of his head and he captured her nipple again, sucking more gently this time, while she moaned in abject pleasure, head falling back so her hair was in the water.

When he finally let her sink back down into his lap, she was trembling and panting. He was so hard against her hip, she thought he must be in pain. Perhaps he was. He was breathing in deliberately measured breaths, and his thighs opened wider to cradle her more deeply against him.

"Do you want me to…" She didn't know what to do. What to offer. But she knew she was dying to touch him.

"I want you to let me do this." His hand slid to catch against the elastic of her underpants. He paused, the fabric pulled far enough from her hip the first ripple of hot water began to caress her bare skin.

Breathless with anticipation, she nodded.

He drew her panties down. The small shift bounced her naked backside against his thighs. Her stomach wobbled at the light abrasion of his leg hair against the sensitive cheeks of her bottom. He pulled the cotton off her ankles and flicked it over his shoulder, joining her bra somewhere in the snow.

"And how does this feel, *süsse*?" His fingertips trailed across her outer thigh to her hip while she absorbed the eddies of hot water moving freely against her most intimate places.

She could hardly breathe. She thought about his touch trailing into those places and shifted restlessly, her nose finding its way into the wet whiskers under his jaw.

"I don't know what to do," she confessed with embarrassment. "I've never touched a man."

"Then by all means, find out what you've been missing." His teeth flashed in a brief smile, but he chucked her chin. "And come here. I want to kiss you again."

She pressed her mouth to his, joyously returning to this wondrous place where she could flagrantly gorge herself on the taste and feel of his lips and tongue and the beard that was rough and silky and utterly compelling.

Shyly, one arm firmly encircling his neck, she let her other hand drift to caress across his shoulder. Those tendons were tight and straining, but not in the way they'd been this afternoon. His pectoral muscles were taut, too, flexing beneath her touch as she dipped her hand below the surface.

Was that his nipple? She scraped her thumb across it, and he made a low sound of pleasure in his throat, one she couldn't help teasing out of him a second time before she shifted to make space for her hand to trail between them, down to the fierce shape pressing so insistently against her hip.

As she closed her fist on the girth of him, his fingers bit into her waist where he anchored her on his thighs. His teeth took hold of her bottom lip, and she felt the rumble of his pleasured groan vibrate in his chest.

How utterly fascinating. She moved her hand, learning the shape of him, discovering what made him hiss or release sounds of delicate agony.

"Am I hurting you?" she broke their kiss to ask.

"No." He stole brief, hungry kisses. "Squeeze tighter."

She looked down at where the dark water obscured her view of him. "I feel cheated."

"So do I." He nuzzled under her chin. Beneath the water, he skimmed his hand along the back of her thigh, but stopped where her leg sat pressed to the top of his.

She tucked her chin and kissed him, squeezed him more boldly and allowed her legs to relax.

His flesh pulsed in her fist and he tilted her, rolling her into a more aggressive kiss that flipped her heart on its edge. Her inner muscles clenched in anticipation, but his fingertips only teased behind her thighs, the barest touch skimming lightly across the fine hairs that protected her folds.

She sobbed with denial. Opened her legs more. Tried to tell him wordlessly what she wanted. He made a low sound of satisfaction and his touch moved to the front of her thighs, stroked inward and upward, until she was the one biting his lip, aching with expectancy.

When his hand finally, firmly covered her, her stomach fluttered and she groaned into his mouth. He seemed to brand her with his intimate touch, claiming her so thoroughly, she had to break their kiss and exchange breathless pants with him.

"If we do this right, we'll do it together," he said in a voice like smoke and velvet. "Yes?"

"Yes," she breathed. Then opened her mouth in a silent scream because he lifted all but one finger from her and gently worked his wicked touch against her.

"Keep stroking me, *süsse*," he urged in a whisper. "I like it. It feels like this." He found the most sensitive place on her body and pressed without mercy, two fingertips now slowly circling to draw her into a place of mindless pleasure.

She shook, groaning with abandon into his naked shoulder, not realizing she had tightened her hold on him until he gave an abbreviated thrust into her grip and made a ragged noise against her ear.

"Like that, yes." His breath hissed with concentrated pleasure. "We're going to kill each other." He rocked his touch, unhurried as he stoked the fire within her. "I couldn't be happier than to die right here, tonight. Like this."

It was the most singular experience of her life, to communicate completely with touch.

To caress him and sense his pleasure as acutely as she experienced her own.

He became her entire world. Nothing mattered in these concentrated seconds except his touch passing across her bundle of nerves, his pulse against her palm, the wall of his iron-hard body shifting with light friction against her skin.

Tension coiled in her abdomen. Through her whole body. She licked his skin and kissed him with abandon, trying to make him understand how exquisite he was making her feel. How he was torturing her beyond what she thought she could stand, yet she never wanted him to stop.

In a subtle move, he hitched her a fraction higher and his touch probed. Her inner muscles tightened at the intrusion of his finger. She shivered despite being so hot she thought she would incinerate. He bit tenderly at her lips with his own, teasing kisses of reassurance as the pressure of his palm rocked where she needed it most.

She saw stars. Gripped him tightly in her fist and matched the rhythm of his thrusts with a lift of her hips against his firm hand.

The crisis rose. She tasted copper and thought she might have bitten his lip. She wasn't sure, but he didn't complain. He only kept up the wild caresses that carried them both over a waterfall so they plunged freely off a cliff into the mist.

CHAPTER FOUR

RHYS VAGUELY WONDERED if there was an aphrodisiac in these waters, because he had never climaxed so hard in his life. Despite aching from the force of it, he wanted nothing but to pull Sopi astride him and sink into the satin depths he'd claimed with his touch.

He gently cradled her trembling body against his unsteady heart, trying to find his breath. Trying to find a shred of sense, because all-night lovemaking had a place—and it wasn't a primordial pond in the frozen wilderness.

With a virgin disguised as a woodland nymph.

He didn't disbelieve her about her inexperience, but he was incredulous that such a passionate woman hadn't found someone to share her sensuality with.

No one has ever made me feel like this.

Him, either, and that shook him. He wasn't entitled to this sort of high. His deepest instincts began to war, one side warning him that he couldn't have this. The other, greedier side wanted to mate and mate some more. Grind himself against her until they were nothing but dust.

She posed a very serious danger, this curious, unassuming goddess of a woman.

He rose abruptly, making her gasp at the shock of cold air on her wet skin.

He twisted to ease her back under the warmth of the water, seating her on the flat ledge he'd vacated.

She blinked in surprise, mouth pouted and shiny from their endless kisses, all but her collarbone hidden from his insatiable gaze.

"I'll fetch you a towel and a robe." He waded out of the water, welcoming the bracing slap of winter frost that cleared his head so he could think.

"You don't have to," she said in a small voice behind him.

"I want to," he insisted, pushing his wet arms into his robe and belting it tightly. "Two minutes."

* * *

Sopi was reeling from what she'd done with the prince. Her whole body tingled with lassitude, the kind that made her want to groan in luxury at how deliciously sated she felt. She couldn't think of any other experience that had left her so dreamily satisfied.

His abrupt departure caused her a pinch of distress, though. The longer she sat here, the more she began to feel self-conscious about her lack of inhibition. About waiting here like a harem girl for the sheik to return.

When she heard his footsteps crunching through the trees, she sat a little straighter, mouth trembling into a shy smile of greeting.

It wasn't him. It was one of his bodyguards. The clean towel and robe he carried glowed like an armload of snow as he approached.

Throat locked, eyes burning in mounting horror, Sopi watched him look indecisively between the soggy pants and shirt she'd left atop her shoes and the snow-covered bench nearby.

"The prince offers his regrets that he couldn't bring these himself. He said he will speak to you in the morning. Um... Here?"

He shook out the items and hung them on the fence, then stepped through the gate and stood with his back to her.

"What are you doing?" she asked, appalled when he stayed there.

"I'm to escort you safely indoors."

Her embarrassment turned to outrage. "I'm fine. *Go.*"

"With respect, I have my orders. Take your time."

She stewed with impotent fury as she realized her choices were to argue while she boiled or end this as quickly as possible. Why was the practical choice always to give in?

And why hadn't Rhys come back himself? Had she turned him off? Had he finished with her already? Was he mad that she hadn't put out with *actual* sex?

Growing more and more horrified by what she'd done, she waded out and shook the robe open, struggling into it without bothering to dry herself. When she scooped up her clothes, she glanced at the thick snow on the far side of the pool and decided to find her underwear in the morning, when it was light.

Moments later, she stomped through the

trees toward her cabin, surprising the body-guard into saying, "Ma'am?" He hurried to follow her new direction.

She ignored him, aware of him trailing her, but she didn't even look at him as she got to her door, unlocked it, then closed it in his face, locking it again from the inside.

With hot, dry eyes and wet, tangled hair, she fell into bed.

Rhys had returned to the deserted spa in time to hear Nanette trying to pull rank on his bodyguard.

"I'm the owner. I can go anywhere I want," she insisted.

"Your mother claims to own it," Rhys had said flatly, moving forward to prevent her from realizing he was coming from the hall-way to the building's exit, not the men's room.

Nanette faltered, frosty expression morphed into welcome.

"That's what I mean, of course. My mother is the owner. Your Highness," she added with a sweet smile especially for him. "When I saw your man standing guard, I wanted to be sure you had everything you need."

"Everything but privacy."

Her smile stiffened, and she looked past him. He waited for her gaze to come back and held it with his most unapologetically imperious glare.

She sniffed and said, "I'll leave you to it, then."

"Do." He waited until she was out of earshot before he muttered his instructions to his bodyguard to take a robe and towels to Sopi, aware Nanette would stake out his floor to see whom he brought back to his room.

Rhys rarely took action without considering the consequences. If he did, he would currently be wondering if a deflowered virgin was incubating a royal baby. He'd had the presence of mind to stay this side of sane with Sopi, thankfully, but he wouldn't expose her as his lover to the likes of Nanette until such time as he'd weighed the ramifications for both of them. What little she'd told him about her relationship with Maude meant there could be consequences for her.

She had also left him with the impression that she was the rightful owner of this property, if not legally, at least morally. Her father had bought it for her mother, who had lovingly restored it, but Maude was the one trying to unload it in a private sale under the radar.

That had his mind churning as he took the elevator back to his floor, passing Nanette in a chair in an alcove, hair twisted around one finger, an open book in her lap.

"Good night," she said as he passed, shoe dangling from her toe.

He nodded curtly, entered his room and went directly to the window on the north wall. He thought he might have seen a flash of movement in the trees but wasn't sure.

Annoyed, he went back to the folio Maude had given him.

Lawyers cost money, Sopi had said.

They did but, as it happened, he had an abundance of both.

Sopi's morning went from bad to worse very quickly.

She woke with the worst type of hangover—the sober kind that piled nausea on remorse with none of the blurry celebration of alcohol to dampen her memory or give her an excuse for behaving so wantonly. She didn't even regret the sex part. She had wanted that, but she felt very much like she'd fallen for a line from a playboy who set up conquests like bottles on a log, simply so he could shoot them down.

At least no one would know, she told herself. Then her walk of shame past the pump house turned up fruitless. One of the hotel's maintenance men must have checked the gate and gathered her bra and underwear. She could only pray her things would be thrown away rather than turned in to Lost and Found.

By the time she was heading into the back door of the hotel and passing Maude's office, her phone was exploding with the usual work-related texts. Sopi had her head down, reading complaints about late deliveries and equipment needing repair, and didn't see Maude waiting for her until her stepmother's haranguing voice said, "Sopi."

Hiding her wince, Sopi detoured into Maude's office. "Good morning."

"Two of Fernanda's friends are arriving in Jasper in an hour. They don't want to wait for the shuttle. Can you collect them?"

"Fernanda can't do it?" Wasn't that the obvious solution?

"She's tied up."

Doing what? Sopi didn't ask. She was too relieved to have an excuse to disappear for three hours. Plus, the drive was always pretty. Minutes later, she was admiring the golden gleam of snow off the craggy peaks above her and caught the stub tail of a lynx as it slunk into the trees.

Maude's information on the women's flight was completely wrong, of course. Sopi wound up with time to kill, so she engaged in retail therapy while she was in the bigger center. Then she sat in the airport addressing as many texts and emails as she could.

When the chartered flight finally arrived, there were a dozen women, too many for Sopi's SUV, *and* they'd already arranged for a private shuttle.

Annoyed, but completely unsurprised—this was classic Fernanda—Sopi drove home alone.

Rhys had grown up on the sort of palace intrigue that had resulted in the murder of his

parents. The infantile game Maude was playing, trying to sell this property without telling the person it would affect most gravely,
was nothing more than a mosquito-like annoyance to him.

Things took a turn into adult parlor games
when Rhys decided to play along while he
turned the tables. He kept hearing Sopi ask,
*How long does it last? What happens when
it's over?*

They had barely even started and couldn't
really continue, not properly. That infuriated
him, but after their intimacy last night, he
couldn't ignore the way Maude was going behind Sopi's back. He was convinced Maude
would pursue the sale with someone else if
he declined, so he decided to go through with
it. He had Gerard call Maude first thing and
tell her to expect the prince's counteroffer
later today.

Rhys then sent his bodyguard to fetch Sopi.
He wanted to come clean about his purchase
and include her in the negotiations. Maybe
they could work out some other arrangement
while they were at it. He knew it was next to
impossible, though, and that put him on edge.

When his bodyguard returned with Cassiopeia's neatly bagged delicates and the news that she had driven away in a company vehicle, he nearly snapped.

This was the only time they had!

He was in a brooding, foul mood when Gerard knocked and entered carrying his trusty tablet. "I relayed the stepdaughter's details to the palace for the due-diligence investigation, sir. You'll want to see this. The palace investigators dug fairly deeply into the Brodeur background—"

"And Maude is on the run from the law?" he surmised facetiously. "Shocking."

"Um, no, sir. Maude and her daughters don't seem to have a criminal record of any kind. But Cassiopeia's mother is a Basile-Munier."

Rhys snapped his head around. "But they died out."

Nevertheless, his blood leaped as he took the tablet and scrolled through the report. It included an image of a birth certificate and a short article by a historian who had visited this spa some years ago. The man had been trying to prove the owner was the surviving child of a prince who had disappeared from public life after an assassination attempt. That prince and his wife had had a daughter late in life. She'd eloped against her father's wishes.

A marriage certificate and a title search on this property all seemed to indicate Sopi's mother was that same woman.

"Is this real?"

"A DNA test would confirm it, although I'm not sure where we'd get a sample. Miss Brodeur seems to be the only surviving member. But if you scroll to the photo at the bottom, it would seem, um, like mother like daughter. And granddaughter."

Rhys stared at a scan of a dated color photograph of two women who both had Sopi's cheekbones and chin, rich brown hair and gleaming dark eyes.

The room was absolutely still and silent, but he felt as though a gust of wind hit him. Went through him. Nearly knocked him on his ass.

This was too easy. Too perfect. This wasn't how life worked. Not how it should do in any case, not for him.

At the same time, a roaring thrill went

through him. He could have her. He *would* have her. His agile brain quickly found the rationale for it. A commoner would have been a fight, but a royal would be accepted without question. Even better, she was a lost princess whose story would pull the spotlight from Henrik. His brother dropping out of public life while he sought treatment would barely be noticed by anyone.

"Forget driving down the price of the spa. I want a swift sale, immediate possession and binding terms."

The checkers game he'd been playing with Maude was flung into the air. This was now grand master chess with a side hand of high-stakes poker.

Within the hour, Gerard had the contract finalized. Maude agreed that the transfer of ownership would remain confidential until such time as Rhys saw fit to announce it. Rhys informed her he would retain all staff but no longer needed a marketing VP or brand ambassadress. The people holding those positions—Nanette and Fernanda—would have to vacate their suite by the end of the week.

"Your late husband purchased this property

for his wife?" Rhys asked as he and Maude set their electronic signatures to the final deal. He was curious whether Maude knew of Sopi's royal blood.

"I understood she had an inheritance of some kind enabling her to renovate it. We rarely spoke about our previous marriages, to be honest. I'm just delighted to finally have this albatross off my hands. I run it as a folly, but it's more work than it's worth."

As Gerard double-checked and pronounced everything settled, Rhys said to Maude, "Would you and your family dine with me this evening?"

"Oh, Nanette and Fernanda would love that."

No mention of Sopi, her considerable contribution to the business or how this sale would impact her.

Maude's complete disregard for her stepdaughter incensed Rhys, making his delight in outsmarting her grow exponentially until a bellow of triumph was nearly bursting from his chest.

It was a warning sign that he felt far too strongly about this. About *Sopi*. If he felt anything, it ought to be the comfortable satisfaction that he had uncovered an opportunity that benefited his brother and was moving strategically to seize it before anyone else could.

Even when he had the spa sewn up, however, Rhys's powerful sense of urgency didn't ease. He tried to pace it off, aware that Sopi would be furious with him, but his deal with Maude was the least of the shocks she would receive tonight.

When Sopi returned and confronted Maude over the wasted day, her stepmother frowned and said, "Oh, you know how Fernanda gets distracted when she's excited. She and Nanette have been invited to dine with the prince tonight. That must be why she mixed things up."

It was a prevarication if not an outright lie. Sopi was dying to say, *Oh, really? Because last night, when I was with the prince, he told me he wasn't interested in either of them.*

But she didn't want to reveal she'd been with the prince. She hadn't felt sordid when it happened, but after brooding on it all day, she was convinced she'd behaved like those women he'd spoken of so disparagingly. The ones who straddled him whether he wanted them to or not.

She went about her afternoon checking in with staff and pitching in as necessary. When a handsome young man approached her as she was covering the booking desk, she smiled in greeting, caught off guard when he used her full name, not the *Sopi* on her name tag.

"Cassiopeia Brodeur?"

"Yes." This was more the type of man she ought to aim for, she thought absently. He was polite and well dressed, but his attitude didn't scream wealth and privilege. He returned her smile, but with polite reserve. He didn't move the needle on her body temperature one millimeter, which was delightfully unthreatening if a little disappointing.

"Please call me Sopi. How can I help you?"

"I'm the prince's assistant, Gerard. This is for you." The small envelope he offered was imprinted with the royal crest.

Her heart tripped, and she ducked the envelope below the edge of the desk to hide how her hands began to tremble.

"Thank you," she said in a strangled voice, cheeks scorching. She wanted to glance around guiltily but held his stare and her smile even though it began to feel forced.

"He asked if I could also take your number?" He offered his telephone with a contact already started in her name.

She balked. Rhys had gotten her naked last night, then fobbed her off on his bodyguard when he was finished with her. She wasn't up for a do-over, if that's what this was about.

"Perhaps if you read his message," Gerard suggested, correctly interpreting her mutinous expression.

She withdrew the card, which was a single sheet, not even folded. It was some kind of high-grade linen stock in ivory with raw edges, also embossed with his crest.

His fine-tipped pen had dug in deep and left small trails, as though he'd rushed to write his brief message, barely lifting the pen. Or had written it in anger.

Where the hell did you go today?
Dinner.
No excuses.

Splotch went the ink on the final dot.

She bit her lip and slid the card back into the envelope, glanced at Gerard.

"Seven p.m. in the dining room with the rest of your family? I'll tell him you're confirmed?"

The rest of her family? *Yech.*

He must have read her reaction. "If there are any impediments, please bring them to my attention so I may iron them away."

She resisted asking him to squash her family flat.

"I'll be there," she said, not sure if she was telling the truth. At least she'd bought a new dress today, still stinging over the incident with her stepsisters. The new one wasn't designer or flashy by their standards, but it had come from an upscale boutique and cost more than Sopi's weekly earnings. She had planned to return it on her next trip to Jasper.

"Excellent. And would you be so kind…?" He offered his phone again.

She hesitated, then gave him her number. He tried it, smiling when a ping sounded in her pocket. "Please let me know if I can assist you in any way."

Perhaps he could offer her some strategies on facing the prince after last night?

For the rest of the afternoon, every time she tried to think up a reason to cry off the dinner invitation, she touched the card in her pocket and could hear Rhys's deep voice warning, "No excuses." Why did she find his profanity-laced impatience so reassuring? It brought a secretive smile to her lips every time she thought of it.

At five fifty-five, Maude called her. "Sopi. We have a disaster in the kitchen. You'll have to run out or breakfast won't happen tomorrow morning."

Here was her excuse to skip dinner, but a devilish part of her refused to seize it.

"We're expected to dine with the prince this evening, aren't we?" she asked with a full pound of smugness. "I had a note from him, personally inviting me. I don't want to be rude."

A pause that was loud enough to *thunk*. Maude might have swallowed. "I assumed you would decline. You tend to set yourself apart from us."

Oh, was it was *her* who did that?

Actually, maybe she did. She had never forgiven Maude for keeping her father in Europe or for spending all his money. Still, Sopi pulled the phone from her ear and scowled at the screen. Maude was sounding particularly petty about a simple dinner invitation. Was she that embarrassed of her unrefined stepdaughter?

"Well, tonight I'll join you," Sopi said cheerfully. "Since it's not often I get a chance to dine with royalty." She hung up and stuck her tongue out at the phone.

Then she suffered a churning stomach for the next hour as she showered and dressed. Her hair, which she never bothered to cut because she always wore it up, was ridiculously long, falling to her waist. At least it had a hint of wave, but it tickled her lower back, where her new dress had a circular cutout.

The dress was a sleeveless knit with a high collar, but it made her look fuller in the chest than she was, which balanced hips that were a shade wider than her stepsisters' fashion magazines told her they ought to be.

She wasn't much for makeup, but her cheeks were pale with nerves. She gave them a swipe of blusher and painted her lips with a pink gloss. She hadn't thought about new shoes when she'd been shopping today so she had only the plain black pumps she wore when she played hostess in the dining room.

As she went onto tiptoe in the bathroom, trying to see her bottom half in the mirror, the butterflies in her stomach turned to slithering snakes. She was kidding herself. Not only would she not measure up to Nanette and Fernanda, she would look downright foolish in everyone's eyes, trying so hard to impress.

Just as she started to kick off her shoes, however, Gerard texted that the prince was sending an escort for her.

Sopi choked on her tongue, texted back that it was unnecessary and decided to do what she'd been doing for years now—brave things out for one more day.

She had put up with Maude's proprietary orders and her stepsisters' snobbery because the alternative was to cede the territory to them and wind up with nothing. Cassiopeia's was her home. She would fight for it to the bitter end.

Which came sooner than she'd expected.

What happens when it's over?

It would never be over. Rhys had found the woman he would marry. The knowledge should have afforded him nothing beyond a contented sense of completion. He didn't like the gnawing sense in him that he needed to leap and snatch and hold on tight. Gerard had assured him Sopi had promised to join them for dinner, but she had become so important to him in the last few hours, Rhys feared that if she wasn't in the dining room when he got there, he might well devolve into shedding blood.

He stalked from the elevator across the short bridge that overlooked the foyer below to the dining room reservation desk. He was as combat ready as any of his ancestral knights, vibrating with a drive to claim.

The babble inside the dining room went silent as he appeared. Everyone rose with a muted shuffle of chairs. A small pocket of women stood to the side of the reception desk. One of them was backed into a corner behind a potted palm.

The tension in their small group hit him like a battering ram, but the sight of Sopi's drawn cheeks and bravely lifted chin reached out to claw into his chest.

"Ladies," he greeted.

Sopi stiffened and skimmed her gaze to a distant corner, refusing to make eye contact.

"Your Highness," the rest murmured.

So. They'd told her about the sale. And she was taking it badly.

Rhys kept an impassive expression on his face, but he wanted to catch her by the chin and force her thick lashes up, so she looked directly into his eyes. He wanted to ask how she dared let these women take advantage of her. Didn't she realize who she *was*?

No. She didn't. Steps had been taken to bury it too deeply.

He had thought to make a dramatic announcement here in the dining room, but as he read the angry hurt in her, he realized he couldn't spring it on her like that. She would hate and blame him a little longer, but he could withstand it.

Any guilt Rhys might have experienced for his underhanded actions in buying the spa dried up, however. It was past time Sopi learned the truth about her mother and herself. He couldn't wait for the transformation.

Maude's younger daughter demanded his attention by stepping forward and offering a curtsy with a breathy, nervous giggle.

"Your Highness, some of my friends have just arrived." She waved at a long table with a half dozen women down either side, all looking his way with anticipation. A few empty seats had been saved in the middle. "We wondered if you might enjoy a more lively evening? They're anxious for a chance to meet you."

"Another time." He glanced impatiently at Maude.

"Of course," Maude said smoothly. "We have a quiet table reserved at the back. Sopi?"

"This way." Sopi didn't smile, and her voice was cold and pointed as an icicle aimed at the middle of his chest. She led the way through the staring crowd.

Ingrained protocol nearly had him offering an arm to escort Maude and her eldest daughter, but he shunned them at the last second, moving ahead of them, all his attention on the sensual swish of loose hair across the top of a stunning, heart-shaped ass that swayed provocatively as she wound her way between the tables.

Dear God, that *hair*. How dare she hide such a thing from him? It was an instant fetish he would need a thousand nights to indulge.

It was a good thing the place was filled with mostly women, because if he caught any man, even one of his lethally trained bodyguards, checking her out, he would duel to the death.

He gritted his teeth, trying to suppress this unwelcome surge of possessiveness. Where was it coming from? It was more than his innate preference to act on his decisions the minute he made them. It was positively primeval. It was an aspect of that wildness he knew lurked in any human, and he didn't like it. He only hoped it would ease up once he knew she was his. It had to. Otherwise they were doomed.

He was given the position at the head of the table, Maude on his right, Nanette on his left. Sopi sat on Maude's right and glared at Fernanda, who shrugged across at her in a silent, *Don't blame me*.

"I want to thank you for your hospitality," Rhys said as their champagne arrived and was poured. "I'll be leaving tomorrow."

"You won't stay the week?" Maude murmured, but she was drowned out by Fernanda's, "Us, too, in a few days. Finally!" Fernanda raised her glass.

Sopi choked strongly enough they all lowered their glasses. Her eyes glimmered as she shot hard looks at each of them.

"You suck. You all suck," she croaked.

There was a collective gasp from tables nearby. Maude said a sharp, "Sopi! Consider who you're speaking to."

Rhys said nothing, pleased to see she possessed a spine after all. She would need one.

"*All* of you." She rose and glared directly at him with betrayed hurt sharp as the edge of a knife.

Her hand jerked, but before she could fling the contents of her wine at him, Rhys's bodyguard caught her wrist.

"Stand down," Rhys barked at him, also rising.

Sopi shrugged away from the bodyguard's hold and stepped away from the table. She threw her glass to the floor in a shattering statement.

"Go to hell. Every single one of you." She stalked out.

"*Someone* doesn't know which side her bread is buttered on," Nanette said into her champagne.

"True," Rhys bit out, sending Nanette a dark glower that made her blanch. He set his hands on the table to lean over the three women. "Those who betray others to get what they want should expect the same treatment. Skip the meal and start packing. Be gone by midnight."

"What—"

He ignored the women's cries of shock as he straightened and sent a curt nod to Gerard. His assistant would ensure the staff were notified that Maude and her daughters no longer gave the orders and, in fact, were no longer residents of the hotel.

As the buzz of gossip and speculation

spread like wildfire through the room, Rhys jerked his head at his bodyguard to lead the way to Sopi's cabin.

How stupid could she get? She had genuinely thought her worst humiliation was allowing a man with more experience to talk her out of her clothes and take a few liberties with her person. She had thought letting down her physical guard where his sexual intentions were concerned had been the careless act, but no. Last night's dalliance had been some kind of misdirection so she would be blindly ignorant of what Maude was really doing.

What *he* was doing. Of course he wasn't interested in her. He had toyed with her the way some executives spun fidget spinners while brokering a deal.

The pressure in her chest threatened to crack her breastbone, but Sopi refused to scream or cry or release any of the aching sobs branding her throat.

Fine, she'd been thinking for the last twenty minutes, after Fernanda had spilled the beans that Maude had definitely meant to be de-livered a few days from now, no doubt after ordering Sopi to load their damned luggage for them. Maude had hissed in warning and Nanette had said, "For God's sake, Fernie. Mummy told you it's confidential."

"What?" Fernanda had had the gall to cast it as a good thing. "She'll be happy. Mummy sold it all to the prince. We'll all be out of your hair by next weekend. You should be happy, Sopi."

Sopi had been utterly speechless, standing there in shock as the prince arrived and everyone stared. She had moved on autopilot, only feeling reality hit her as they reached the table. Instead of holding a chair for their guest the way she would as a hostess, the prince's assistant, Gerard, had moved behind her and held her chair.

It had been so unexpected, it had knocked her out of her stasis and into a plummeting realization that everything had changed. The one dream she had clung to was gone. The only home she had ever known would never be hers.

The nascent fantasy she had had that a prince—a damned royal *prince*—might see something in her beyond a penniless chambermaid had burst like a bubble, leaving her coated in a residue of disillusion and humiliation.

Slamming into her cabin, she kicked off her shoes. Hard. So that one dented a cardboard box and the other went flying toward the bathroom door.

She wrenched at the dress she'd bought with him in mind. It was meant to be pulled on gently to retain the shape and prevent snags in the delicate knit. She dragged roughly at it. Tried to tear it because she hated it. She yanked it off and dropped it where she stood and wiped her feet on it. She was panting and shaking, still trying to catch her breath after her sprint through the snow-laden trees, filled with an endless supply of *hate*.

With a final twist of her foot, she flicked it to the side and shoved at a stack of boxes, freshly delivered this afternoon and left for her to move to a more convenient location. Everything was always left to her to do, and she was *sick* of it. She shoved the stack even harder, so it fell with a tumble.

The crash wasn't nearly as satisfying as she had hoped, especially when it was followed by a loud stomp of a heavy foot leaping onto her stoop. The door flung open to let in a burst of cold air that swirled like a demon around her nearly naked body.

Him. The instrument of her ruin.

"Bastard," she muttered and turned away to take her narrow stairs two at a time.

Below her, she heard the door click closed. She glanced down from the loft and gripped the rail with humiliated rage as she watched him take in the clutter and the mess of boxes. He picked up her dress and gave it a light shake.

"Come right in," she said scathingly. "Act like you own the place."

He lifted his gaze, and she instantly felt naked. Not just physically, which she mostly was, but as though she was utterly transparent. As if he could see through her sarcasm to those puerile fantasies she'd spun in her head. It was so agonizing to be seen this way, she had to hold back a sob and turn away. She yanked out a drawer in her dresser, digging for jeans and a pullover. The stairs creaked as she stuck her legs into her jeans.

He appeared in the loft and flicked his gaze

in harsh judgment of her used furniture and what she had always thought of as a cozy living space. As her turtleneck nearly choked her, and she yanked at her hair enough that it had some slack outside her collar, she saw the loft through his eyes and was mortified to realize it wasn't humble. It was shabby.

Angry that he was seeing it and forcing *her* to see it, she said, "I was being facetious. What I really meant was get lost."

What she really meant were two words she had never said to anyone, no matter how badly Nanette had ever baited her, but she was feeling them this evening. She really was.

He draped her dress over the footboard of her bed. "We'll continue this discussion in my room."

"Gosh, I would love to accommodate you, Your Highness, but I have to pack and find a place to live. Because if you think I'm going to work for you, you need to see a psychiatrist about your loose grasp on reality."

"My people will pack for you. Socks," he said, nodding at her bare feet.

"I'm not going anywhere with you."

"*Süsse*, I will carry you out of here kicking and screaming if I have to. We are not talking here."

"There is nothing wrong with the way I live." Everything was wrong with it, but she would die on the hill of defending what was left of her home after the way he had treated her. "This is what a person has to do when they're kicked around by people who have more power than they do."

"I know that!" he shouted, then seemed to pull himself together with a flex of his shoulders and a clench of his jaw. "It reminds me of the way my brother and I lived when we were in exile. I hate it. I won't stay here, but you and I will talk. Am I carrying you?"

Shaken by that completely unexpected admission, she only hesitated long enough for one brow to go up in a warning that he was dead serious.

She swallowed and told herself she was only cooperating because this was too small a space for the explosive emotions still detonating inside her and radiating off him. She found a balled-up pair of socks and sat on the top stair to put them on with her boots, aware of him looming over her the whole time.

"I don't know what we could possibly have to say to one another," she muttered.

"You will be surprised," he promised in a dark vow. He followed her down the stairs and out the door.

His bodyguard flanked them as they crossed to the hotel and blocked anyone from joining their elevator.

Sopi refused to make eye contact with the wide stares that came at them from every level of the foyer.

"I forgot my phone," she murmured as she realized her hands and pockets were empty.

"It will be retrieved." He let her into his suite himself, waiting while the bodyguard moved through in a swift check of all the rooms. Rhys stationed the man outside his door with, "Only Gerard, and only if the place is burning to the ground."

"Yes, sir."

Rhys let out the sort of breath that expelled hours of tested patience.

Sopi hugged herself and moved to the window where she noted he had quite the view of naked women frolicking in the pool below.

"I was in here last week," Sopi murmured. "Packing Nanette's and Fernanda's things to move them down the hall so you could have this suite. Except that's not what I was doing, was I? You've all been cooking this for ages, and I just did the heavy lifting so they could be on their way faster."

"If they're still here in three hours, I'll set them on the stoop myself."

Taken aback, she realized that whatever fury she was nursing, he had plenty of his own. "If you're so angry with them, why—"

He held up a hand to stop her, pausing in removing his suit jacket before finishing his shrug. He threw his jacket over the back of a chair and loosened his tie on the way to retrieving stapled documents from a stack on the desk.

He dropped one set onto the coffee table. "That's a copy of the offer Maude accepted today." *Slap.* "That's the transfer of Cassiopeia's into your name."

CHAPTER FIVE

"WHAT?" STUNNED, SOPI stepped forward in shocked excitement, unable to believe it. She pulled up as she realized such a thing would have to come with conditions. Her excitement drained away. "Why?" she asked with dread, fearing she already knew.

His beard darkened where he bit the inside of his cheek. His irises glowed extra blue and laser sharp as he branded patterns on her skin with his gaze. "Last night, you asked me where this was going."

"It's not going anywhere. You made that perfectly clear when you didn't come back to the pool afterward." Her heart hammered in her chest.

"Nanette was loitering in the spa. I was protecting you by sending my bodyguard."

"Sure you were," she choked. "That's also what you're doing here, I guess?" She waved at the paperwork.

"I am," he said in a voice so gritty it left her feeling abraded all over. "Nanette knew I was with someone last night. I could have revealed you, but I wasn't ready to. I wanted time to consider exactly how I would answer your question."

"And this is your answer?" She was growing more appalled by the second. How did he manage to hurt her so easily? So *deeply*? Despite last night's intimacy, they were still virtual strangers. He shouldn't be able to impact her like this. "You went behind my back to cut a deal to buy my *home*?"

"I wanted to talk to you about it." Her temper didn't faze him. He stood as an indifferent presence, unrepentant and untouched. "You weren't here. From now on, you're not allowed to be angry with me for actions I take if you don't show up to hear my side of it before I take them."

"Wow. Sure," she agreed, laying on the sarcasm with a trowel. "I will be sure to never be angry with you in future when I *never see you again*."

"Dial back the histrionics. We have a lot to cover, and you don't want to peak too early."

Her blood boiled. She shot her arms down straight at her sides, hands in tight, impotent fists.

"I have a right to be angry, Rhys! You bought property stolen from *me*." She jabbed at her chest. "Now you want to gift it to me like you're doing me a favor—" Her voice caught, but she forced out the rest, each word like powdered glass in the back of her throat. "But I expect you want favors in return, don't you? Virginity is quite the precious commodity these days, isn't it? You make me sick!"

She turned to wrench at the door latch, but he was on top of her, surrounding her and catching her hand in a firm but strangely gentle grip as he caged her. His deep, velvety voice growled into her hair, causing tickles against her ear that made goose bumps rise on her nape.

"It's a wedding gift."

"To who!" She tried to shove her elbow into his gut.

"You." He spun her and pinned her to the door. "Now settle down before my bodyguard bursts in here and I have to kill him for trying to touch you again."

"You really have lost half the cards from your deck. I'm not marrying you." She pressed her forearms against his chest, forcing space between them, so astounded she didn't have the sense to be intimidated. "We've known each other two *days*. Why would you even suggest such a thing?"

"Because the gradual approach is not open to me." His jaw clenched as he studied her flushed, angry expression.

She didn't want to be aware of his heat and weight pressing into her, but she was. She really didn't want to *like* it. She turned her face to the side, resisting and rejecting.

"You were going to come to my room last night. Weren't you?" His voice was smoke and mirrors, casting a spell she had to work to resist.

"If you had come back to the pool and asked me yourself, I probably would have, yes." She lifted her chin but winced internally as she admitted it, hating herself for that, too. "Were you planning to propose if I had?" she scoffed.

He backed off a fraction. "I wasn't thinking much beyond how badly I wanted you in my bed."

"That's a no, then." She gave him a firm nudge, but he was immovable.

"Everything changed while you were playing hide-and-seek this morning."

"I was doing my *job*." Her voice faded into a discouraged sob that rang in her chest as she realized she no longer had one of those.

He sighed and gave a comforting brush of his thumb against her jaw. "Maude was determined to sell the spa, Sopi. Someone else would have bought this property if I hadn't. Be happy it was me."

"You people need to quit telling me how to feel about this." A burning ache of blame stayed hot in her throat.

"Don't lump me in with your stepfamily," he warned, not even flinching. He only grazed her cheekbone with his fingertips as he tucked a wisp of hair behind her ear. His voice changed. Gentled. "And hear what I'm saying. Your life would have toppled regardless. Whether you're happy about it or not, I'm offering you a cushion. A velvet one. With gold tassels."

His words, edged in irony, held a quiet finality that shook her to the core. Her world *was* shattered. All she had known had been upended and was sliding beyond her reach.

Her heart began to tremble and she pushed harder on his chest, freshly angry, but scared now, too. "Let me go."

He waited a beat, then stepped back and dropped his hands to his sides, watchful.

She hugged herself, moving into the room to put space between them so she could think, but she remained too anxious and confused to make sense of any of this. Marriage? Really?

"I've always thought that if I were to marry, it would be to someone I love. Someone I *trust*. I'm not going to marry to get a *thing*. Especially not to get something that should already be mine."

"I wanted you to be here while I negotiated with Maude." He sounded brisk but tired as he moved to the bar and poured two glasses from a bottle of whiskey that was already open. "If it were up to me, I would have hired the lawyers you needed to fight Maude, taken a partnership in the business in exchange, but there was no time. Plus, all of my business dealings are scrutinized. I can't foot the bill on a stranger's legal fight—or gift a hotel to a woman with whom I am having an affair— without causing a lot of questions to be asked. Buying this property as a present for my future wife, however..."

She shook her head, unable to take in that he really meant that.

Nevertheless, a distant part of her was processing that *she* would finally be the boss here. All her friends would have secure jobs. That was as important for the village as for the spa. She grew dizzy with excitement at the prospect.

But why her?

"Is this like a green-card thing or something?" she managed to ask. "Would it be a fake marriage?"

He snorted as he came across with the glasses. "Not at all."

"You're genuinely asking me to marry you. And if I do, you'll give me this hotel and spa, all the property and rights to the aquifer. Everything," she clarified.

"If you'll live in Verina with me and do

what must be done to have my children, yes," he said with a dark smile.

She was still shaking her head at the outrageous proposition but found herself pressing her free hand to her middle, trying to still the flutters of wicked anticipation that teased her with imaginings of how those babies would get made.

She veered her mind from such thoughts.

"Why? I mean, why *me*?" She lifted her gaze to his, catching a flash of sensual memories reflected in the hot blue of his irises.

"I've already told you. I want you in my bed."

"And that's it? Your fly has spoken? That's the sum total of your motivation?"

His eyes narrowed, becoming flinty and enigmatic. "There are other reasons. I'll share them with you, but they can't leave this room."

That took her aback. "What if I don't want to carry your secrets?"

"You're going to carry my name and my children. Of course you'll keep my secrets. Would you like to tell me yours?" He regarded her over the rim of his glass as he sipped, as though waiting for her to tip her hand in some way.

She shrugged her confusion. "I'm not exactly mysterious," she dismissed. "The most interesting thing that's ever happened to me is happening right now. You realize how eccentric this sounds?"

"Eccentric or not, it's a good offer. You should accept it before I change my mind."

She snorted. "You're quite ruthless, aren't you?" She spoke conversationally but knew it as truth in her bones.

"I do what has to be done to get the results I want. You understand that sort of pragmatism, even if you've pointed your own efforts in dead-end directions. I look forward to seeing what you accomplish when you go after genuinely important goals."

"This is my *home*. It's important to *me*."

"Then claim it."

A choke of laughter came out of her. "Just like that? Accept your proposal and—" She glanced at the paperwork. "I'm not going to agree to anything before I've actually reviewed that offer."

"Due diligence is always a sensible action," he said with an ironic curl of his lip. He waved his glass toward the table, inviting her to sit and read.

Gingerly, she lowered onto the sofa and set aside her whiskey.

Rhys kept his back to her, gaze fixed across the valley as he continued to sip his drink, saying nothing as she flipped pages.

His behavior was the sort of thing a dominant wolf would do to indicate how little the antics of the lesser pack affected him, but she was glad not to have his unsettling attention aimed directly at her as she compared the two contracts. Aside from the exchange of money on Maude's—and the fact that hers finalized on her wedding day—they were essentially the same.

"I want possession on our engagement. *If* I decide to accept your proposal," she bluffed, fully expecting him to tell her to go to hell.

"Done. On condition we begin the making of our children on the day our engagement is announced." He turned, and his eyes were lit with the knowledge his agreement had taken her aback. "We'll keep the conception part as a handshake agreement. No need to write that down in black-and-white."

He brought her a pen. His hand was steady as he offered it. Hers trembled as she hesitantly took it.

"Are you completely serious?" she asked.

"Make the change. Sign it. I'll explain why I want you to marry me. You'll accept my proposal, and Cassiopeia's will be yours."

Inexplicable tears came into her eyes. This was too much. Too fast.

"What if we get engaged and I back out?"

"I expect you to go into this with good faith, Sopi. I will."

And he expected her to sleep with him. Get started on making his babies. She might not have the option of backing out on their marriage if that happened.

She wanted to sleep with him. That was the unnerving part. Not for Cassiopeia's or a wedding ring or babies. For the experience. To be able to touch him and feel...

She swallowed, hearing him say her life would have changed regardless. He was right about that. Which made her stupid to turn this down. It was probably the best outcome she could anticipate. Her alternative was to let him have Cassiopeia's while she tried to sue Maude for a slice of the purchase price. Good luck with that. Maude was headed out of the country. Sopi would most likely lose any settlement she won to lawyer fees anyway.

She told herself she was only signing as a matter of hearing him out, not really committing to changing her entire life.

Shakily, she made the change and set her signature to the page, feeling so overwhelmed her head swam as she rose to bring the pages and pen to him.

He set the contract on an end table and inked his name next to hers, handing it back to her for her inspection.

She moved away from the intensity of his gaze, trying not to think about the full severity of what she was edging toward. She returned the document to the coffee table and picked up her drink, took a bracing sip of scorching whiskey.

"The floor is yours, Rhys." The alcohol left a rasp in her voice. "Tell me what sort of husband I'll get for the price of a spa."

"No more sarcasm," he said flatly and threw back the last of his drink, then went to pour another. "I offer more than a damned spa in exchange for marriage. You'll have security of every kind. Wealth and power and a type of fame that can be tiresome but has its uses. It can be very effective when used for altruistic acts. I thought that might interest you." He cannily noted the way she swung to face him.

"Why would you think that? You don't know me." She demurred, forcing her gaze elsewhere while she took another nervous sip.

"I know more about you than you do," he said with a cryptic sort of confidence that made her feel as though the floor shifted beneath her. "You want this place because it's your home, not to develop it. You care about your employees and work alongside them because they're your friends. You never ask them to do a task you wouldn't do yourself. In fact, you look after complete strangers better than you look after yourself."

"I'm just trying to keep the place running." She shrugged off his compliment.

"You're self-effacing and self-sacrificing. You'll need that."

"Being nice doesn't mean I'm ready to have children." If she was quick to help others, it came from being bounced into friends' homes when her father had traveled, which had happened frequently. She had learned to pitch in to fit in and be welcomed.

When her father had remarried, she had thought he would finally stay home and they would live more as a family. Maude had had expensive tastes, however, and his business had been declining, forcing him to travel even more. What Sopi had really learned from the humbling experience of losing everything was the importance of ensuring she could offer support and attention to her children before making any.

"If I could give you more time to absorb all of this, I would, but time is a luxury I no longer have. My brother has testicular cancer. It was discovered when he and his wife failed to conceive."

"Oh." She swayed, knocked back by the news but wanting to move toward him, to offer some sort of comfort. "I'm so sorry."

He was steely and still, his frozen demeanor holding her off. She stayed where she was.

"What...?" She didn't know what to ask, how to respond.

"They're pursuing treatment options right now. Obviously, we hope he will survive, but even if he does, he will almost certainly be sterile. I'm next in line, therefore I need an heir. And a spare. Turns out they have their uses," he stated with grim humor.

He sipped, and she copied the motion, stunned to her toes.

"Are you aware of Verina's history?" he asked. "Support for my brother has never been higher, but we still have a handful of detractors looking for a foothold. We can't afford any show of weakness. I have to take action to secure the throne before any of this comes to light."

As whiskey slid down her throat like a rusty nail, she glanced at the contract she'd signed.

"I see the urgency, but I still don't understand why me? I mean..." She had to clear her throat to speak, not wanting to state baldly that he might become king. She certainly didn't want to picture herself at his side if he did. "You're, um, saying your son or daughter is likely to rule Verina. There are thousands of blue bloods to choose from as a mother for those children. There are a hundred in this *building* right now." She waved at the walls.

"True. And I came here expecting to find my bride among those women." He tilted the last of the liquid in his glass. "I'm expected to marry someone with that sort of pedigree." He was eyeing her in that penetrating way again. "Henrik's wife, Elise, is the daughter of a diplomat, schooled much as all the women here." He waved at the walls. "But her father lacks a title, and it was a long, hard-won fight for Henrik to be allowed to marry her."

"Then—" That made her a poor choice, didn't it? She suddenly felt as though the floor was falling away, leaving her grappling with such profound disappointment, she realized that she *liked* the idea of marrying him.

"I don't personally care about bloodlines. If I must marry, I want a woman who will be honest with me and show some integrity, rather than tie myself to someone like your stepsisters. I would much prefer to share my bed with someone I want to share my bed with," he added pointedly.

The hot coals in the pit of her belly seemed to glow bright red, as if he'd blown on them, sending heat through her limbs and up into her cheeks and deep into the notch between her thighs. Her scalp itched and her breasts felt tight.

"I don't even have your sister-in-law's education," she said. "I'm as common as clover. You really want to fight that hard for sex?"

He didn't laugh or reassure her that yes, he wanted her *that much*. Instead, his expression turned even more grave.

"You're not a commoner." He spoke with matter-of-fact solemnity. "Your mother was the daughter of Prince Rendor Basile-Munier. He tried to retake his principality of Rielstek when the USSR fell apart. There was an attempt on his life, and he fled to Sweden, where he lived out his days."

He spoke so confidently a jolt went through her. It evaporated into a pained sense of setback. Of stinging anguish that this marriage really wouldn't happen.

"Someone has been embellishing." Regret

sat as an acrid taste in the back of her throat. "Did you overhear a local gossiping? I've never heard names and details like that, but it's pure nonsense."

He cocked his head. "Why do you believe that?"

"Because I would know if my mother was a princess! Instead, I know when and how that rumor got started. A guest claimed to be writing a history of some kind. He asked my father if my mother had been a princess. My father said that, like most writers, the guy had a screw loose. Mom would have told him if she was secretly royal. Even though it wasn't true, I was young enough to be taken by the idea. I told some staff, and it turned into a joke. It's a sort of urban legend, something employees repeat to prank the tourists. It's not true, Rhys."

"Yes, it is," he stated. "That historian was an extremely well-regarded academic. I studied from his textbooks myself. Unfortunately, he passed on before this particular work was published. That's why our staff had to dig to find it and why your heritage isn't common knowledge."

"No." She shook her head, growing agitated. "My mother would have told me. My father would have known."

"Not if her father had actively tried to bury their identity, worried for their safety."

"No, Rhys."

"The property in Sweden is still in your family's name. The caretakers live rent-free. They had no incentive to reach out, but they have provided some documentation to our palace investigators. Our team is looking for a means of DNA testing, but they're quite satisfied with the evidence they have so far—especially once they compared photos from your social media pages to your grandmother."

He took out his phone and showed her a photo of a woman in a tiara and a sash. She could have been Sopi dressed in costume.

Sopi dropped her glass, having completely forgotten she was still holding it.

Thankfully, it only held half an ounce of liquid and didn't break. She scrambled to retrieve it and shakily set the glass next to the contract she had signed. *The one agreeing to their terms of engagement.*

She shoved her butt onto the sofa cushions and set her face in her hands, concentrating on drawing a breath while the whole world spun in the wrong direction, pulling her apart.

"I didn't think you were aware," he commented drily.

"This can't be true, Rhys. Does Maude know?"

"I didn't tell her. If I gave a single damn about her, I would look forward to her reaction when she realizes I'm making you my wife and that any future regard you bestow upon her will be strictly on your terms."

Sopi was convulsively shaking her head. "I can't marry you. You can't really expect me to move to Europe with you? Turn into a princess overnight?"

"I've just explained that's what you already *are*." There was no pity in his voice. "I'm exactly the sort of husband you were meant to have."

"But you can't *want* me! I—"

"I damned well do." He sat on the chair to her left, only one hip resting there so he was crowded into her space. His knee brushed hers, and he forced her hands down so she had to lift her gaze to his. "I've explained what's at stake for me and my country. Hell yes, I want to engage myself to a lost princess. We'll be the feel-good media storm of the year."

"You expect me to tell people?" It was another blow she hadn't seen coming. She was going to have a bruise on her forearm where she kept pinching herself, trying to wake up.

"Of course I do. You're ideal."

"No, I'm not!" She waved at the bargain jeans and top she wore.

"You will be."

"You're not listening to me!"

"I've heard every word. You're shocked by ancestry that has been hidden from you. You're already homesick because this place is your connection to your parents. You're afraid to become my wife because it feels bigger than you ever expected to be."

"I'm afraid of *you*." She realized she was trembling. "How can I trust you when you're forcing all these things onto me?"

"I'm only giving you what you're supposed to have. Do you want to tear that up?" He pointed at the contract they'd signed.

No, but she didn't want to accept that she had no say over anything, not even who she *was*.

He drew a long breath that tried to neutralize the charged energy between them. "I'm just the messenger, Sopi."

"You're proposing to be my *husband*. Maybe you're fine with marrying a stranger, but I'm not." She was a stranger to herself, and it was so disconcerting her brain was splitting in two.

"We're not strangers," he scolded in that tone that crept past her defenses like wisps of drug-laced smoke, filling her with lassitude.

"Sure, you know everything about *me*." She was trying really hard not to become hysterical. "All I know about you is that you swim naked and get whatever you want!"

He let that wash over him, then snorted as if he found something in it funny. He drew a breath and rose, nodding in a way that suggested he was conceding a point.

He pulled out his phone, said, "Gerard. We'd like the dinner we missed. When do you expect Francine? Good. Send her up. I want Sopi to meet her."

"Who?" Sopi asked as he ended the call.

"The new manager of Cassiopeia's until such time as you make changes."

"This is happening too fast, Rhys."

"I know." Now, he almost sounded as if he pitied her. He stepped closer and cradled her jaw, giving her cheekbone a light caress with his thumb. His hand felt a lot warmer than her face.

Despite being wary of trusting him, she rested in that reassuring palm. She wanted to throw herself into his arms. He was the only solid thing in a crumbling universe.

Murmured voices outside the door had him releasing her to invite a middle-aged woman to enter. She had a sleek blond bob and an elegant figure in a crisp suit. If she was jet-lagged, she didn't show it a bit. Her handshake was firm, her smile friendly. Her English held an accent similar to Rhys's, somewhere between French and German.

"Francine will be your proxy once our paperwork is finalized and you take possession," Rhys said with a nod to their contract.

"I'll take the first week to observe, then communicate my recommendations." Francine mentioned her credentials, which were stellar. "I've taken possession of the office and all the equipment. I thought to also start an audit, if you agree?"

Sopi glanced at Rhys. "I can't afford her." Maybe after a year of penny-pinching, but not when Maude had just drained the coffers dry.

"You can," Rhys assured her. "Once the press release about us goes out, this place will thrive. Go ahead with the audit," he instructed Francine.

Sopi's chest felt compressed. Agreeing to hire Francine felt like an acceptance of marriage and all the rest.

"Francine will ensure future profits will continue to support her well-deserved but exorbitant salary. Even if you were going to be here, I would recommend you move forward with her as your manager."

I will be here, Sopi wanted to argue. She couldn't hold his unwavering gaze, though. Her eyes were growing too hot and damp.

"We'll come back in a few months," he offered in a gentle coax, as though trying to soften a blow. "The ski hill has accepted my offer to purchase, but they want to finish the season. When I come back to finalize that, you can check in here."

It was a thin lifeline, but she grasped it. "You promise?"

"I do."

She gave Francine a timid nod, pretty sure it was the equivalent of pushing the button that would blow up her bridge back to her old life. Even though it was already on fire.

Francine smiled and departed, revealing the room service trolley had arrived. The bodyguard wheeled it in before returning to his station outside the door.

More out of habit than anything, Sopi began transferring the dishes to the small dining table.

Rhys was right there to help. She stepped back, startled to find him so close. "I can do it."

"So can I. I've waited tables."

"When?"

"When I had to." His mouth pursed and his movements slowed as he took care with the setting of their cutlery. "I've been through this sort of transition, Sopi. Both directions. I wasn't given time to pack a bag or hire staff or worry about anyone beyond myself and my brother."

He spoke in a distant tone, as though consciously removing himself from painful memories.

"Online it says you were ten when the revolution happened. I don't understand how anyone could break into a home and commit violence against innocent people."

"Power is an aphrodisiac. The justification was that my father did nothing for Verina. It wasn't until he was gone that people realized the difference between a leader who serves his country and autocrats who take from it."

She couldn't tear her eyes from his grim face.

"I'm so sorry. How did you cope? Where did you go?" He hadn't had any velvet cushions to land on.

"There's a small lake on our border with France. Some of the servants were escaping in a rowboat and took us across with them. We were taken into a protective custody by French authorities, but several governments squabbled over us through those early years, all eager to wage war on our behalf. The real goal was to take possession of Verina, not that we understood it at the time. We only wanted our parents. Our own beds."

"Are you saying you were political hostages?" She was appalled.

"Pawns. Well-treated orphans on whose behalf they claimed to operate. Eventually, a Swiss diplomat who had been a close friend of our father's was able to take us in. He saw to our education with a focus on politics so we understood what was happening to us and Verina. We quickly realized the only help we should accept from any government was the basic human right to move freely. Henrik was sixteen, I was fourteen when we finally moved out on our own."

"That's when you lived…"

"Poorly. Yes," he said shortly. "It was a frustrating time, some of it typical adolescent rage, but we were realizing how badly we'd been used. That the people who should have helped us were operating from their own motives. The greater loss was hitting us, as well. We were mature enough to see the damage that had been done to all of Verina. The path forward to repair not just our own lives, but those of people who we were meant to protect and lead, was daunting. I honestly don't know how Henrik faced being the one. We were eating out of dented cans, barely making the grade at school because we were working any spare moment we had just to pay rent on a moldy apartment. He proved himself to be worthy of the role, though, showing the necessary leadership, making the hard decisions."

"But you were there, supporting him. That had to be important, too."

"To some extent, I had to become what we both hated. A gambler and a hustler, playing politics and digging at social cracks. Eventually, protesters in Verina forced a proper election. When the legitimate government was reinstated, we returned. Then we had to find our feet as royals all over again in a very different environment."

"Are there still detractors? Are you in danger?"

"No worse than any other dignitary. In fact, we're quite popular, having lived as the common man. We're seen as an inspiration. Plus, we brought prosperity back to Verina. Henrik's resumption of the throne after the conflict makes him an emblem of our country's resilience. We have to work hard every day to maintain stability and goodwill, though."

That stability was under threat by his brother's illness. Rhys had so much to carry—dark memories and concern for his brother and responsibilities to live up to. She searched his face, wondering how *he* managed.

"I didn't tell you all of that to downplay what you're going through. I'm saying I can be your guide as you move from being a hidden royal into the spotlight. I've done it. I know the pitfalls and how to navigate them."

"Why can't I just stay here and be…me?"

"Is that really what you want?" His frown of disapproval struck particularly deep. "After learning all that is available to you, all that is yours *by right*, you want to continue scrubbing floors? Is that who you are, Sopi? A coward?"

CHAPTER SIX

"COWARD!" SOPI REPEATED STIFFLY, flinching and looking away, then lifting her lashes to throw a scold at him. "I'd think you were above name-calling."

Rhys took it as a good sign that she wasn't curled on the sofa weeping, but on her feet, consistently pushing back while taking most of this on the chin.

"Peer pressure, *süsse*," he mocked lightly.

"Not funny."

"It infuriates me that your grandfather was unable to retake what ought to be yours," he admitted with anger he would always struggle to suppress. "I've been there. I want you to fight for what belongs to you."

"You do see the irony in that statement, I hope?"

"I refuse to apologize for buying this property. It was cheaper and more expedient than hiring lawyers. Less public, too." He drew out a chair for her. "Maude will get her come-uppance in other ways. Sit. Eat. Digest," he suggested drily.

"I don't—" She cut herself off and grumbled, "I'm not hungry."

"So we'll get to know one another and you'll begin to trust me."

After a brief hesitation, she gave a shaky sigh of defeat and sank into her chair.

Rhys stayed behind her, his attention caught by the loop of hair that had been teasing him ever since she had dragged this turtleneck over her head in her squalid little cabin.

He gathered the mass in his fist and gently tugged. She stiffened, then leaned forward so he could work the tresses from inside her shirt. When every last strand was free, he combed his fingers through it, pleased when she shivered in reaction.

"You'll speak to me before you ever think of trimming this," he ordered.

"Even what I do with my hair is up to you now?" Her voice quavered.

The fractures in her composure were showing after all. He wound her hair in a rope around his fist and set a light kiss on her crown.

"That was the teasing demand of a lover, *süsse*. Don't take it so much to heart."

"We're not lovers."

Everything in him wanted to contradict her. Prove to her in the most basic way that the chemistry between them meant that their engaging in a physical relationship was as inevitable as their marriage.

But he heard the tremor of fear that underlay her bravado. Her remark about being unable to trust him had been a slap in the face. He was doing what he could to buffer her from the sharp edges of her new reality, but she was still being knocked around by it.

"We're not the sort of lovers I want to be. The kind I hope we will be very soon." He released her hair so it fell down the front of her shoulder and over the swell of her breast, then set his hands on her shoulders, noting the tension in her, much like an animal ready to bolt. "I'm not going to force you, though. You can relax."

Her shoulders softened slightly, and he thought he glimpsed a pout of consternation on her lips when he released her and moved to take his chair across from her. Mixed feelings? That was progress, at least.

"I do need an heir, though," he reminded her, glancing at the wine in the bucket. The bottle was open and ready to pour. He drew it out and gathered the moisture with the towel.

She choked on a humorless laugh, one that said she had given up. When he glanced back at her, she was staring at him through eyes that glimmered with tears.

"It will be okay, Sopi. I promise you." He poured lightly since she'd already had whiskey.

"What would it even look like? Marrying you?" She gulped before they'd toasted. "Besides the fast track to making babies."

"The wedding or the marriage?" He held his glass for the clink of hers. "Both will brim with protocol and adherence to tradition, I'm afraid, but we'll carve a personal life out of it. Henrik and Elise manage to." He set aside the dish covers, releasing an aroma of sage and roasted apple as he revealed slices of elk with risotto and creamed spinach.

"Would we divorce if it didn't work out?"

"I never undertake anything with a mind-set that I'll fail. Short of a catastrophic betrayal, let's agree we'll make every effort to work out our disagreements. But divorce is legal in Verina, if it comes to that."

"And the baby?" she asked as she picked up her cutlery.

"Babies. Plural, if we might be so blessed. What about them?"

"*Would* you see them as a blessing? Or are children merely something you're ticking off a list? Like 'wife.'" Her gaze was admonishing, but that wasn't why he flinched.

Losing his parents had been the most painful experience of his life. The mere thought of losing Henrik was sending fractures of agony through him. Children were sheer emotional peril, something he would have avoided forever if he could.

"I've always been ambivalent about having children," he prevaricated. "I've met enough in my travels to know they can be moody little brats, but they can also be quick to offer unconditional love to a complete stranger."

"They're like tiny humans that way," Sopi said drily.

"Indeed."

She had relaxed a little. Humor had returned the sparkle to her eyes.

He was tempted to take her hand, make a move, but forced himself to sit back and give her space to relax.

"I was leaving the raising of progeny to Henrik. Aside from not being particularly anxious to marry and not wanting to overshadow him by having children before he did, he was always a more paternal man than I saw myself to be. Maybe that was my impression because he was my older brother and made all the decisions for us in those early years when we lived on our own. He very much wanted children with his wife. Elise wants a family very badly. This has been a terrible blow for both of them. I'm torn up taking this action," he admitted heavily. "It feels like a betrayal to them both."

"Will that affect how you feel toward your children?"

"No," he dismissed with confidence. "I don't know what sort of father I'll make, but I would try to emulate my own. He was caring. Busy and firm and he set very high standards, but he was encouraging and capable of humor and affection. I miss both of my parents every day."

"Me, too. My father worked away a lot, but when he was home, we were always laughing and he was proud of any ribbon or test score I brought home. He talked about me running Cassiopeia's as though it was a given, never saying anything like, *When you marry*, or suggesting I needed a man to look after me."

"Did he never want to bring you with him?"

"He offered to send me to school in Europe. I had my friends here. I think we both thought there would be time later to connect." She twirled her glass, mouth pulling to the side. "There wasn't."

"No," he agreed pensively. Time, that bastard, loomed like a vulture over everyone. "How do *you* feel about children?"

"I guess I pictured myself with a family eventually. I always wanted a brother or sister, so I've always known if I had children, I would have at least two or three. It bothers me that my parents aren't alive to be grandparents, but I miss *having* family." Her mouth tried to smile, but the corners kept pushing down.

That was, perhaps, the thing that terrified him most about his brother's diagnosis. What family would he have if Henrik wasn't here?

He had to reach out then, offering his hand with his palm up, but it wasn't a pass. It was comfort and a desire for it in return. Recognition of affinity.

"I think we've found something I can give you that you truly want, Sopi. I will take care of your children very well. I promise you."

"I believe you, but what about—" She looked at his hand, her own still clinging to her cutlery, knuckles white. "Do you think... Please don't laugh, but I always thought I would be in love when I got married."

Ah, love, that priceless gift that could exact too much.

"I've never been in love. I can't claim to be capable of it." Like every other intense emotion, he was wary of it. "I believe we will come to care for each other, though."

"I don't know if that's enough." She set

down her knife and fork. "I'm really scared, Rhys."

"I know."

"But I don't want to be a coward."

"Being afraid doesn't make you a coward. Giving in to fear does. Bravery is pushing forward despite the cold sweat."

"Peer pressure again?"

"You *are* my equal." If not a mirror image, at least a complementary piece that promised a greater sense of wholeness. He hadn't expected to find such a thing, ever.

In fact, it unnerved him to some extent, niggling at his conscience. He reminded himself this marriage was for Henrik and the crown, not himself.

"Trust me," he cajoled. "And I'll prove you're my equal. *You* will."

She bit her lip. Her hand hovered over his so he felt the heat off her palm radiating against his own. He made himself be patient, not reaching to take despite his craving to grasp and squeeze.

Very slowly, the weight of her soft palm settled against his.

He closed his hand in a possessive grip, experiencing a leap of something in his blood. Conquest? Or something even more profound and basic, like finally coming up for air when he thought he was drowning?

He breathed through it and brought her hand to his mouth, setting a light kiss on fingers that went lax with surprise.

"Welcome to your new life, Princess."

Rhys sent her to bed alone, which left her feeling ambivalent. She tossed and turned, waking unrested to the discovery this hadn't been a dream. They ate a light breakfast and she was given a memo to sign advising the staff that she was the new owner, that Francine was the manager and they should proceed with business as usual.

Then she was given a copy of the press release. It announced her as the recently discovered Basile-Munier princess, stateless but newly engaged to Prince Rhys Charlemaine of Verina. She would take up residence in the palace of Verina with her fiancé immediately.

"Leave your phone with Gerard. He'll field all those messages," Rhys said as her dated smartphone began percolating like a boiling-over pot. He frowned at her clammy, nerveless fingers and warmed her hand in a reassuring grip. "A new one will be waiting for you in Verina."

And then what? She almost wanted to say, *Shouldn't we go do that thing now?* They had a handshake agreement, didn't they?

Rhys seemed intent on getting to Verina first. Aside from the bellman, who kept his eyebrows in his hairline as he loaded their luggage into the helicopter, Sopi saw none of the staff or her friends. She gave the bellman a weak smile and a wave before all that she knew fell away below her.

She had never flown before but knew right away that the jet they boarded out of Jasper was not the average commercial experience. Rhys waved her into an ivory-colored leather recliner against a window and took the one next to her. They were served fresh coffee in bone-china cups that rested on a polished mahogany table that unfolded from a concealed cupboard. A large-screen television was muted but ran the news with market numbers tracking across the bottom of the screen. Rhys handed her the remote and invited her to watch anything she liked.

Rhys's assistants and bodyguards remained in the cabin at the front of the plane, in seats that faced the galley and were closed off from this more luxurious area.

That was when Sopi began to see how different her life would be. Ironically, she felt shut out of the place where she belonged, rather than ushered into a higher sphere.

Through the flight, Rhys talked in a dozen languages to a multitude of people. Gerard came back several times to request her approval on things she had no business approving. When they stopped in New York to refuel, a stylist came aboard with half a dozen outfits.

By the time she landed in Verina, she no longer recognized herself. She wore a sheath with a forget-me-not print that had been altered to fit her perfectly. A pair of low-heeled sandals finished the sweetheart look.

When Sopi rejoined Rhys from the stateroom, hair and makeup elegantly disguising how pale she was, he glanced up, did a double take, then clicked off his phone and set it aside.

"You look lovely."

"Thank you," she said shyly. "I feel like an actress in a costume." Playing the part of a woman who said, "Gosh!" and fell out of trees while rescuing kittens.

"The trick is to own the role. If you believe it, everyone will."

"Are you acting?" she asked, unsurprised when his mouth twitched and he said a decisive, "No."

She hadn't thought so. They began their descent, and her stomach knotted so tightly she could hardly breathe.

"Don't be nervous," Rhys said, reaching across when she wrung her hands in her lap while they drove from the airport. "They're surprised by how quickly this is happening, but pleased. Elise is very down-to-earth. You'll like her."

Meeting a king and queen was the least of her nerves. She was *engaged*. She had taken possession of Cassiopeia's. That meant she had to follow through on the rest of her agreement with Rhys. What if she was bad at sex?

What if he lost interest after the first time? What if she didn't get pregnant? She had so many what-ifs floating in her head, she couldn't articulate them.

They were shown directly into the formal receiving parlor for the king and queen. The sun was coming up, piercing through a stained-glass window to cast prisms of light around the couple who had risen early to greet them.

Henrik was in his early thirties, a clean-shaven version of Rhys. His innate vitality belied any hint of illness. His wife, Elise, was a delicate blonde with a warm smile.

"Why don't I show you around the palace," Elise said after a few minutes of innocuous conversation about Canada. "I'll help you get your bearings, then leave you in your room to rest."

Sopi shot a look at Rhys. He gave a small nod to indicate she should go with Elise, but her ears were already burning, certain she was being removed so he could speak freely about her to his brother.

"I'm not the storyteller our butler is. Do ask Thomas to take you around when you have a free hour. He conducts the tours when we open the palace and gardens for public viewing in the summer," Elise said.

The main floor of the palace consisted of a grand ballroom, the throne room, a cavernous dining hall and a veranda that overlooked gardens and the lakeshore. Elise pointed to a green door. "Panic ensues if we go below, so try not to."

But that's where I belong, Sopi wanted to protest. Once again, she experienced the sensation of being shut out of her own life. Her real one.

She clasped her sweaty palms together, lips pinned closed while she mentally searched for the words to tell Rhys he'd made a huge mistake. That *she* had.

Elise took her up a wide flight of stairs, where she waved negligently toward one wing. "Our residence. Your room is next to Rhys's." She waved in another direction, where maids were scurrying to move boxes stacked in the hall into a room with open double doors. "Still unpacking. Best to stay out of their way a little longer."

"Unpacking?" It was the first time Sopi had

spoken. Her voice cracked. "I only brought one suitcase." Rhys had said the rest of her things from the cabin would follow shortly.

"Rhys said you needed a wardrobe. Those are from my usual designers. My assistant arranged it. The stylist will help you source more."

Sopi felt sick. This was exactly the laissez-faire attitude her stepsisters had taken, buying clothes on someone else's tab that they might never even wear. Sopi couldn't—wouldn't—become like them.

She looked back the way they'd come, pretty sure she could find her way to where Rhys was still meeting with his brother.

"Come. I want to show you my favorite place. I think you'll like it." Elise led her through a door and up a set of spiral stairs that climbed a tower. When they stepped outside, they stood on a wall that overlooked the lake.

The view was breathtaking. A light breeze picked up Sopi's hair and caressed her skin, soothing her ragged nerves.

In a way, it even looked like home with the lake and the surrounding mountain peaks.

Verina was a small country, but it packed exquisite scenery into every square inch. As they slowly paced to the far end, the quaintest of villages came into view, one with stone bridges and red roofs and the tall spire of a church. Beyond it, the grassy hills were dotted by patches of snow and grazing goats.

"This is where Henrik proposed to me the day he was allowed back into Verina. He brought me straight up here before showing me anything else. He said he wanted a good memory to replace the one he'd left with. Do you know how they left?"

"I read about it. It's tragic." Her heart still ached for Rhys.

"It is," Elise agreed. A poignant smile touched her lips as she gazed across the valley. "They lived with us for a while."

"Your father is the diplomat who helped them?"

"Rhys told you that?" She studied Sopi openly.

"He was trying to bolster me, explaining that he hadn't always lived like this. I wasn't born into this sort of life. It's very...overwhelming."

"It can be." Elise nodded thoughtfully. "Did he also tell you why he's rushing you?"

Sopi bit her lip, nodded. "I'm really sorry about Henrik."

She half expected Elise to be angry that Rhys had revealed their private heartache, but Elise only looked anguished and maybe a little relieved not to have to relay the details herself. Her worried gaze switched to the distance.

"They're very close in their own way," Elise said, adding in wry warning, "It can be annoying. They grouse at each other over insignificant things, refusing to talk it out properly. Men." She rolled her eyes. Sobered. "They're fiercely protective of one another, though. It's amazing. To a point. Henrik is worried about him." Now her face was nothing but hollow shadows. The cords in her neck stood out with stress.

"Henrik doesn't think I'm good enough for Rhys." Sopi clasped her suddenly aching stomach. "It's okay. I don't think so, either."

"That's not what I'm saying at all." Elise caught her arm, her grip strong. Urgent. "I'm asking you for a favor. I want Henrik to be confident that Rhys can handle all he faces, otherwise Henrik will step in and try to carry some of his burden. I know that Rhys is taking on a lot. He'll have to cover Henrik's duties to the throne, arrange a wedding. Then he'll have a wife and the making and rearing of children. It's so much to ask of you both. *I know that.* But this is the man I love. He's all I have."

She wouldn't even have Henrik's child. That grief was a dark knowledge lurking in the backs of Elise's eyes. Her anguish twisted up Sopi's conscience so she instantly wanted to ease her mind any way she could.

"Henrik is opting for a very aggressive treatment. It will give him his best chance at surviving, but he needs to give all his focus to getting through it."

"Of course," Sopi murmured. This poor woman had enough on her plate without Sopi whining about having won an ancestral lottery and not knowing how to handle it. "Of course, I'll do whatever I can. I understand the stakes, perhaps not as intimately as you do, but I know how important it is that this marriage take place and—" result in babies

"—work. I know Rhys and I have to project the best possible image."

"Thank you." Elise drifted her eyes closed with relief and gratitude. "I wasn't sure if... But Rhys is a very good judge of character. I should have known he wouldn't attach himself to someone who would put her interests ahead of others."

You're self-sacrificing. You'll need that.

She smiled weakly, wondering if the reason she was ideal was less about her blue blood and more about her willingness to shelve her own needs in favor of others'. She was realizing she had done that to her own detriment in the past, but how could she switch gears now? As it turned out, this king and queen weren't a pair of demigods demanding to be served. They were a couple in love who faced a heart-wrenching situation. Sopi genuinely wanted to do anything she could to ease their suffering.

Even if it meant sleeping with a man she barely knew.

Sopi's liquid-eyed glance as she followed Elise from the room stayed with Rhys as his brother remarked, "You're moving very quickly. I expected you to bring her here for further discussion, not drop it into the press as you left the tarmac."

They had stayed on their feet after the women left, both given to pacing during heavy discussions.

"You disapprove of her?" Rhys's hackles went up.

"I don't know yet," Henrik stated with characteristic frankness. "You have to marry, Rhys. That's a fact, but I expected you to explore your options. How could you know within two days that she's the right one?"

"Look at who she is."

"Oh, on the surface, she's perfect. I heartily agree the spectacle of her background works to my advantage. I'm talking about a more personal connection, though. Wouldn't you rather marry someone you care about? *Love?*"

"Not a requirement for me," Rhys rejected bluntly. "I believe Sopi and I will have a very comfortable arrangement in the long run."

"Comfortable," Henrik scoffed. "That's your aspiration for a life partner?"

"I don't wish to be moved by greater forces," he said truthfully, still uncomfortable with the compulsion that had drawn him toward Sopi in the first place.

"You don't want a marriage like mine?" Henrik folded his arms, frowning.

"No one will ever have a marriage like yours." Rhys smiled with sincere fondness for his sister-in-law. "Elise is one of a kind." If there was such a thing as soul mates, Henrik had found his. Because of that, Rhys was as concerned for Elise as he was for his brother. "How is she coping, now you have more information?"

Henrik let out a weighty sigh. "Exactly as she always does. Brave and stubborn and deaf to anything but the outcome she is striving for." Henrik was wry, yet his voice grew unutterably heavy. "I hate myself for doing this to her."

"It's not your fault."

"I still question everything I've ever done." Henrik poured himself fresh coffee, then ignored the cup. Squeezed the back of his neck.

Rhys knew the feeling. Was Henrik's diagnosis a rebalancing of scales for some action Rhys had or hadn't taken? He desperately wanted to believe there was some way he could take control of what was happening and change it.

"I should have convinced her to move on years ago," Henrik said. "If she was married to someone else, she would have the children she wanted by now."

"She doesn't want another man's children." The doctor had floated the idea of using Rhys's sperm, but none of them had been comfortable with that proposal.

No, Henrik had declared. If Rhys's heir would inherit the throne, his brother ought to be married to the mother of his child.

"If Elise was capable of loving another man, that would've happened by now," Rhys said. "I don't know why she's so enamored. You're not as charming as you think you are," he chided. "But she loves you blindly and unfailingly."

Henrik sent him a look of reproof at the insult but nodded agreement. "It's true. I'm luckier than I have a right to be. Happier, too. That's why I want this for you." He turned on the head of a pin, switching from humbled husband to imperious monarch and domineering older brother in the space of a breath. "This life is hard enough. The wrong partner could drain you dry. You want someone by your side who strengthens you. You won't find that with a stranger, Rhys."

Henrik's words caused an unsettled sensation in Rhys's chest. The flip side of caring that deeply was a carrying of the other's pain—*in sickness and in health* went the vow, didn't it? Rhys didn't want the sort of agony his brother and sister-in-law were currently going through, but he couldn't voice that apprehension.

"Sopi is more than meets the eye," he said instead.

"She's up to *everything* that might be asked of her?" Henrik was obliquely referring to taking the title of queen, should it become necessary. "If Elise didn't love me the way she does, she would have left this life a long time ago. Do you realize that, given your plan for a quick engagement and marriage, you're going to have to play the star-crossed lovers who couldn't wait? Is she up for *that*?"

Rhys had realized that. There wouldn't be

any announcements about Henrik's condition until Rhys was married with a baby on the way. Typically, a royal wedding would take a year of planning. His and Sopi's would happen a couple of months from now. Six weeks, if they could manage it. Their engagement party would be organized as soon as possible.

"Love at first sight," Rhys declared with an unconcerned smile. "Sopi and I will sell it. Don't worry about any of this. Concentrate on getting through the treatment. For all our sakes. I want my brother, and I want my king."

Henrik grumbled an agreement, and they turned to other things.

CHAPTER SEVEN

SOPI NAPPED AND woke disoriented, desperately needing reassurance. Rhys was tied up with the king, though. When she did hear from him, it was a message from Gerard requesting she dress for a hastily organized, informal dinner to meet Verina's prime minister and a handful of other dignitaries.

Informal it might be, but Sopi was put in a full-length off-the-shoulder velvet gown. It was such a dark shade of indigo it was nearly black. Subtle ruching ensured the otherwise straight fall of sumptuous fabric accentuated her curves, and a slit at the back allowed her to walk. Dozens of shoes had been delivered, and she stepped into a silver pair with mirror-finish heels before moving toward the lounge between her room and Rhys's.

Nervously, she knocked, then entered when she heard him call, "Come in."

He was nursing a drink but lowered his

glass as he took in her appearance. Her heart soared at the sight of him in a white jacket with satin lapels and a black bow tie. His beard was freshly trimmed, his demeanor so quietly powerful, he seemed to reach out and grab her from across the room while remaining untouchable himself. Unattainable.

"You look stunning." His voice was as smooth and rich as the satin-lined gown that caressed her skin as she moved.

"Thank you." Her hair had been wound onto her head in a crown, and she self-consciously touched the amethyst pendant at her throat. "These are beautiful." The weight of the matching earrings told her they hung in her lobes, but she still wanted to clasp them to ensure she hadn't lost them. They were one more extravagance she wasn't comfortable accepting. "Can we talk about...all of this?"

"After dinner? Our guests will arrive any minute. We should be downstairs to greet them." He set aside his drink and came across to offer his arm. "You don't have to knock," he said as he led her from the room. "This is your home. By the time we're married, we'll have taken over this entire wing."

About that, she longed to say, but they were approaching the top of the stairs, where Henrik and Elise had just arrived.

Sopi subtly squeezed Rhys's sleeve as she practiced the deferential nod she'd been taught by the protocol coach. They followed the couple down to the formal receiving room.

They spent the next few hours dining and making small talk with people who acted pleased to meet her, but Sopi wasn't so naive she didn't know she was more a curiosity than anything else.

Through it all, Rhys remained a watchful presence, within touching distance yet rarely touching her. Sopi was intensely relieved when the evening concluded and they retreated to their lounge.

"Be honest," she demanded as he closed the door. "How bad was that?"

"I thought it went well."

"Really? Because every time I looked at you, you were… I don't know. Displeased?" Distant. Aside from offering his arm, he'd been completely hands-off when she had been longing for a sign of approval or affection. Acceptance.

"I would have stepped in if you were floundering. I thought you handled yourself beautifully." He poured fresh drinks.

"Then why are you so…" She studied his guarded expression as he brought her a nightcap. "Tense," she decided. "Like you're trying not to yell at me or something."

His brows went up. His mouth twitched, and some of the stiffness in his expression eased to amusement.

"It's not that type of tension, Sopi. My mind has been elsewhere most of the night." His gaze slid to the door to his bedroom.

Her scalp prickled. All she could say was a faint, "Oh."

He sipped. His gaze was full of laughter at both of them, causing pulls of attraction in her middle.

"I'm really nervous," she admitted into her glass. "Maybe once it's over with, I'll relax."

"Over with." His humor disappeared in a flash of something more feral. "You're not anticipating our lovemaking?"

"I don't know what to expect, do I?"

His expression softened slightly. "I told you

I won't force you. If you have misgivings, let's address them."

She opened her mouth, but nothing came out. All she could see was the obvious love between Elise and Henrik. They weren't heavy with pet names or physical affection, but their smiles at each other were very natural. They glanced at each other frequently and seemed to read each other's thoughts. It spoke of a truly special link—the kind Sopi would have wanted for herself if she'd known such a connection was possible.

"Sopi?" Rhys prompted.

She crossed her arms, not wanting him to think her juvenile with her romantic longings.

"Every time I want to complain about what's happening to me, I think of what your brother and Elise are going through. Then I feel petty. But I always thought my stepsisters were petty, presuming that the world would simply provide all they needed. Dresses and jewelry and fancy dinners." She fiddled with her pendant. It wasn't the whole of her reservations, but it was a big part of them.

"You're not like them," he assured her. "You won't become like them."

"You'll stage an intervention if I show signs?"

"The minute you deliberately flash your cleavage to get a man to break out his wallet, I will draw you aside for a lecture, I promise you." A dangerous, smoky edge imbued his tone.

"Now you sound possessive." And there was no reason she should find that titillating.

"I am," he stated without apology. "It's another reason I want to address any concerns you have. Once you're in my bed, I will be highly resistant to your leaving it."

Until the deed was done? That thought made her melancholy. She realized her feet were protesting the heels and sat to remove them.

"Everything is so *big*, Rhys. I'm twenty-two. I should have room to make mistakes at this age. Date the wrong man and get a little drunk in public." She had barely touched her wine at dinner, terrified of becoming clumsy or loose tongued. "No one this young should get married to anyone."

"She said with wisdom beyond her years." He shrugged out of his jacket and loosened his tie. "This *is* a lot of pressure, Sopi. I'm not going to tell you you're wrong to feel it and struggle with it. The fact that you're aware of the downside of your new position, not blinded by the shine, tells me you're smart enough and strong enough to handle what you face."

"Every time I try to tell you I'm wrong for this, you tell me I'm right," she grumbled. "I'm afraid you only want to marry the person I'm supposed to become, not the person I *am*."

"They're the same person."

"No, they're not!"

"They are," he insisted. "Listen, if you want me to tell you where you're failing, I will. You're limiting yourself," he stated bluntly. "Think bigger. Let yourself grow."

"I can't!"

"Why not?"

"I don't know!"

She hung her head in her hands, embarrassed that she was acting so childish, yelling like a toddler. She didn't even know where her reluctance to reach higher stemmed from. Maybe that stupid audition tape?

She lifted her face, frowned with self-deprecation as she realized that probably was it.

"When I was fifteen, I made a tape for a singing show," she admitted. "It was a lark with a friend. We weren't serious, but I made it to the top ten, and the organizers wanted to fly me to Toronto."

"That doesn't surprise me." His expression cleared at the switch of topic. "I heard you in the sauna the other night. You have a lovely voice."

Had it only been some thirty-six or forty-eight hours ago that they had kissed and groped each other in the hot pool?

She shrugged off the compliment, mumbling, "Thanks, but it felt like a fluke. It was exciting, though. I started thinking bigger." She gave him a doleful look.

"You wanted to sing? Professionally?" She saw the wheels turning in his head, trying to assimilate this information with the path they were on. "What happened?"

"My father died. I had to bow out, and I was too sad to try again. I think I felt safer staying home. Staying small." She hadn't put

that together until now, but she saw how il-
logical it was to let that experience hold her
back. "Maybe I'm still feeling that way."

"I completely understand how losing a par-
ent stunts your growth." He came to sit across
from her. "I don't judge you for it. But you
have essentially been running Cassiopeia's.
And you were doing it without any real support. That's no small task." His expression
grew introspective as he studied her. "I'm not
surprised those promoters saw something in
you. You possess initiative and determina-
tion and star quality. One way or another, you
were destined for greatness, Sopi."

She shook her head, dismissing that.

He didn't argue, which left her hearing his
voice echo in her head. Somehow that held
even more impact.

She thought of the sense of expectation she
had felt from Elise earlier. From everyone,
starting with the maid who had asked what
time she should wake her, to the text from
Gerard confirming her schedule for tomorrow.

People wanted things from her—they always had. In fact, she had to wonder if Maude

had begun putting everything on her plate because Sopi had stepped in to take the lead every time her stepmother had attempted to.

Ugh. Maybe Rhys was right and she had been putting all her efforts into micromanaging in a misguided effort to take the control she instinctively desired.

She scowled at him, starting to think maybe he did know her better than she knew herself.

"Did you always believe you would get back here after you were exiled?" she asked.

"I did," he said with simple honesty. "I had to. I couldn't..." He squinted as though looking into the past. "I couldn't accept that my parents' lives had been lost for no reason. That's why I was angry when we lived so poorly. I couldn't believe that our parents had given their lives so we could live like that, barely surviving. Intellectually, I know life can be cruel and not every wrong is righted, but I had to believe the wrong against us would be corrected. It was the only way I could get through my grief."

She nodded thoughtfully. "I accept that this has to happen. I do. I want to stop fighting it, but I think I'm mourning my old life. Do you ever pine for that simpler time?"

"Occasionally," he admitted. "I miss the pleasure of listening to a live band while pouring beer behind a bar, not filtering every word through the lens of political impact. You're the first person to make me feel like that man again, if you want the truth. As though the veneer is unnecessary. I don't have to be anyone but myself. I can swim naked," he summed up with an ironic smile.

But you're you, she wanted to say. His air of confidence and control wasn't a veneer. It was an innate part of him. She didn't have anything like it.

Rather than protest, however, she basked in the quiet knowledge that she offered him something no one else did. What would he give her, though?

A sudden hollow sensation in her heart made her smile wobble. She longed for the things every human yearned for: passion and emotional bonds and intimacy.

"What if the sex is awful?" she asked with tentative anxiety.

The corner of his mouth dug in. "The sex

will be fantastic. You'll have to trust me on that. Until I prove it," he added slyly.

Her inner muscles clenched in a most telling way, causing heat to flood through her. She didn't ask about the rest, but surely if they were talking like this, and shared their bodies, the rest would manifest?

"Okay," she murmured.

He cocked his head, arrested, gaze locking onto her while his whole body seemed to gather like a predator about to pounce. "You want to go to bed? Right now?"

"I'm starting to realize I'll be scared either way, so yes. I think so."

"You're scared of me?" His head went back and his narrowed gaze flashed with something she couldn't identify.

"I'm terrified of all of this," she said with a wave of her hand. "Who you are. How you live. How you expect *me* to live. But I'm realizing that I can't let fear hold me back. I have to confront it."

He swore and looked to the ceiling. Started to speak. Took another moment to find words.

"I don't want to say no to you, Sopi. I want you in my bed *right now*. But not as some sort of bravery challenge. I want you to *want* to be there. With *me*."

"I do!"

"Do you?" he challenged. "Who do you want to sleep with? The prince or the man?"

"The man. The warm body. The hands that erase all the frightened thoughts from my head," she admitted baldly.

After a long moment of consideration, he stood and held out one of those hands, palm up with invitation. "I can do that."

She set her hand in his. Felt the squeeze in her chest when he closed his grip over her fingers and drew her to her feet.

"I have to know that this much is real, at least," she whispered.

"It's very real." He skimmed a light caress around the shell of her ear and set her dangling earring to quivering. "I want the touch that empties my mind, too. I want that like water and air."

His touch tickled beneath her jaw, inviting her to lift her mouth in offering. She loved the feel of his silken whiskers as she petted along his jaw, drawing him down.

His kiss was gentle—too gentle. She

pressed into her toes, wanting the conflagration to consume her.

He was too strong and easily flexed his muscles to draw back from her. One heavy hand on her hip kept her from closing the distance. He teased her by rubbing his lips lightly against hers, and his breath wafted hotly over her mouth as he spoke.

"This is our first time, *süsse*. I'm not going to race you to the finish line." He slowly eased his mouth over hers again, taking his time as he deepened the kiss.

He didn't have to crush her mouth to inflame her, she realized as she melted under his lazy, thorough veneration of her mouth. She grew lethargic, curling her arms around his neck while she leaned her weight into him, wallowing in the sheer freedom to kiss him the way she'd been dying to since their skinny-dip.

When she had her fingers speared into his hair and his embrace was the only thing holding her up, he lifted his head.

"The world outside our bedroom is always going to be a difficult place, Sopi. Even the world inside a bedroom can be complicated.

My hope is that ours will be a retreat from the chaos. Out there—" He nodded at the door to the hall. "I need the princess who is willing to play a supporting role. That's convenient, but it's not why I want you. In here..." He drew her to the door of his room. "I want *you*. Just you."

Her heart stumbled as she crossed the threshold into the lamp-lit room.

"I always knew that sex would be a step I couldn't take back. I think that's why I held back from taking it." It was another aspect of her fear of reaching too high.

"That's why I don't want to rush you." He stood behind her and found a pin in her hair, gently extracting it. "If you want to slow down or stop, tell me. If I don't have your trust with your body, I don't have your trust at all." His mouth nuzzled against the nape of her neck, and he inhaled, making her shiver in delight.

"I'm worried you'll think I'm silly or dumb."

"We frolicked like otters in a pond. We're past silly and dumb."

She had to chuckle at that, but when she

lifted her hands to help with the pins, he growled a noise of protest.

"Let me do it. There was a comic book in my youth, one with a Valkyrie whose long hair was always hiding the most intriguing curves and shadows on her figure. I have latent fantasies I'm looking forward to indulging."

"Good thing my fantasies run to comic book nerds, I guess."

He barked out a laugh of enjoyment and slipped his arm across her collarbone, hugging her into his shaking frame. "I've been called worse."

She was smiling, hands on the muscled forearm that held her so firmly, cheek tilted into his strong shoulder. A whimsical, wistful happiness filled her. A sense of possibility.

"This is really why I'm here, Rhys," she confided softly. "I don't think I could have lived with wondering where this might have gone."

He turned her in his arms. His face was solemn as he plucked the last two pins that held her hair. He unwound the long braid and surprised her by looping it behind his own neck, leaving the tail against the front of his opposite shoulder.

"Me, either," he admitted gravely, making her stomach lift and dip.

This time when he kissed her, it wasn't slow and tender and gentle. It was hot. Thorough. Carnal. His beard scoured her chin, and his arms squeezed her breath from her lungs. She grabbed the tail of her own hair where it hung against his shoulder and pulled, tying them together while an aching noise throbbed in her throat.

If she thought to be the aggressor, she had sorely overestimated Rhys's willingness to submit. He cupped her head and ravaged her mouth, raking his lips possessively across hers, delving to taste and not stopping until she was trembling.

When he broke away, they were both panting, and he wore a satisfied look as he admired her through half-lidded eyes.

"My only regret about the other night is that I didn't get to see you. Not properly." He turned her and flipped her unraveling braid to the front of her shoulder as he unzipped her. Slowly. Inch by inch, cool air swirled into pockets of heat. Sensitive goose bumps rose on her skin.

"Rhys." Each of her heartbeats thudded in a slow pound of anticipation that made her sway under the impact.

"I've been thinking constantly about it. The smoothness of your skin." He parted her dress at her spine, fingertips tickling into the small of her back.

She arched in pleasure, spears of heat thrown like lightning bolts into her loins by his hot, proprietary touch.

"How you were so shy, then not." He found the clasp on her strapless bra and released it. As it loosened, his caress traced where it had sat, moving forward until he took her breasts in his hot palms. "How your nipples felt against my tongue."

They hardened so quickly, they stung. His thumbs passed over them, strumming such a fierce pleasure through her, she squirmed, pushing her backside into his hips. She immediately felt how hard he was and wriggled a little more enticingly.

"And that," he said in a voice growing guttural. "How you give as good as you get. You made me lose my mind. I didn't behave that wildly as a teenager." He held her nipples in a pinch that hovered on the precipice of pain, keeping her very still as her pulse seemed to ring in each of those points, bouncing off the hard palms that cupped her.

"Losing control like that scares the hell out of me." He scraped his teeth against her nape and thrust into the cheeks of her butt. "I still want to go there with you again."

She covered his hands, unsure if she wanted to stop him or urge him to be more aggressive. He held her in an erotic vise, but all she did was turn her head so he could kiss her. He did, stimulating her until she ached with yearning. She dragged one of his hands down to cup where she was growing damp and distraught with need.

His strong hand stayed there as she rocked, teasing them both until she was shaking with desire.

"You're so close, *süsse*." He nipped at her ear. "What do you need?"

"I don't know," she sobbed. "You."

He growled and released her, turning her and brushing the open dress down. When he nudged her backward, she thought he was helping her step out of the puddled velvet, but he took her farther, until she felt the edge of the mattress against the backs of her legs and sat.

She only wore her panties and found herself knotting her fists in the duvet as she gazed up at him uncertainly.

"Trust me?" he asked.

"I do." She nodded, even though her heart pounded with nerves.

He smiled darkly and pressed her shoulder so she let herself fall onto her back.

"This is what it means to be mine. All of you." He leaned over her to drop a kiss on her chin, her breastbone, little presses of silken beard and soft lips all the way down her middle. Lace abraded her thighs as he stole her underwear while trailing kisses from her navel to her hip bone.

He held her gaze very boldly as he parted her knees and dropped to the floor at the side of the bed. His effortless strength pulled her toward him. Her thighs went onto his shoulders, and she gasped as he stropped his beard on each of her inner thighs, making her shiver with anticipation.

He blew softly on her fine, damp curls, and

she trembled again until the damp heat of his mouth settled with ownership against the most intimate part of her. With a small cry, she reflexively tried to close her legs against the intensity of sensation. She had known what sex was, but she hadn't known it was surrender. Not like this. She would belong to him completely after this. She already did, because she struggled to absorb the onslaught of sensation, but she didn't fight it.

He was in no hurry, taking his time building her tension until she ached all over. She hadn't known that arousal had this ability to consume. She could hardly breathe. Her blood was fire in her veins. Each moment was a drawn-out agony of spearing pleasure that coiled her tighter, and then a pulse beat of eternity waiting for it to happen again.

She lost her ability to speak or form conscious thought. She couldn't process how wickedly good this felt as he swept her with starkly intimate caresses. Arching, writhing, she let the crisis overwhelm her, too greedy for it. Too ready. In moments, she was mindlessly saying his name and shuddering under the force of a shattering orgasm.

A beautiful, floaty feeling came on the heels of it. She didn't have the strength to pick up her head but ran her fingers into his silky hair, trying to convey how lovely he had made her feel.

He didn't stop. He switched from soothing to a fresh, deliberate assault that sent a spear of acute desire twisting through her.

"What are you doing?" she gasped, shocked that she could go from satisfaction to craving in seconds.

"Do it again," he commanded and went back to pleasuring her mercilessly.

"I can't."

His touch penetrated, and the sensations redoubled. She didn't think she could handle it. He tossed her into a place of intense excitement, but her hand in his hair urged him to continue, and suddenly she was soaring again, higher, abandoning any restraint as she released jagged cries of ecstasy.

He soothed her again, letting her catch her breath, but he didn't let her sink into satisfaction. He teased. Made her say his name again so the pleading of it echoed in the room.

He shifted his kisses to her inner thighs,

and she could have wept with loss. Her thighs were still twitching, her skin damp and her heart unsteady.

He rose to set his fists on either side of her hips and tracked his gaze avidly over her naked, trembling form. His face was angular and fierce, his smile savage. "We both needed that."

"Do I…do that to you now?"

"Do you want to?" He pushed to stand straight and yanked a hand down his front to tear his shirt open. "Next time," he decided just as brutishly. "The thought of your mouth—" He squeezed himself through his trousers and hissed his breath through his teeth before he dragged at his clothes to remove them. "Still with me, *süsse*?"

"Yes." She swallowed, mesmerized by the way the lamplight gilded his skin to pale bronze. She had only caught a glimpse of him at the side of the pool. Now, staring at him unabashedly, when he was so close she could touch and he was naked and fully aroused, he made her weak.

He started to reach toward the nightstand, caught himself in his fist again, and his breath hissed through his teeth. "My first time, too, *süsse*. Naked. I don't know if I'm going to hang on long enough."

He came down alongside her, his hand sweeping from her hip to her waist to her rib cage while his mouth pressed against her shoulder.

She felt dazed, not having given thought to what this really was. She flashed her gaze up to his, fearful that this was all simply an act of procreation for him, not the starkly profound union it was for her.

He was watching her, maybe tracking the myriad emotions accosting her. Nerves and desire and something new and sweet were moving through her, feelings she didn't know how to interpret, but that made her feel incredibly vulnerable.

His eyes were glittering with feral lights of excitement, but there was a surprising gentleness in him as he caressed her now. He picked up what was left of the braid in her hair and turned his wrist to wrap it around his hand. When his grip was tucked close to her neck and she couldn't move her head, he kissed her. The light restraint held her captive for his teasing, barely there kisses. Heat flowed into her loins, and she crooked her knee and rolled her hips into his.

He broke their kiss to glance at her knee. "The way you respond will be my undoing." He released her hair and trailed his hand down to claim her mound. His touch delved into slippery heat, making her jolt.

"Too sensitive?" He eased away so he was only cupping her.

"Not enough," she complained, rolling fully into him and taking hold of the taut shape of him. "I've never felt so greedy in my life," she admitted. "I want to know how it will feel, Rhys. I want you inside me."

She found herself on her back, the agile strength of him caging her. It was intimidating, yet she didn't feel unsafe. Not physically. Everything that made her feel secure in life had long spiraled beyond her control, but here, trapped by him, she was safer than she'd ever been.

He shifted atop her, using his strong thighs to push her legs apart. She felt the shape of him, the heat and hardness against her unprotected flesh. He nipped her chin and cupped her breast, then bent his head to take her nipple into the hot cavern of his mouth.

She groaned with abandon, twisting and scraping her hands across his shoulders. "Rhys, I can't take this."

He lifted his head, shifted and guided himself against her. She felt the pressure. The forging stretch of him pushing into her. She gasped. This was way more intimate than she had expected.

He paused. "Let me see your eyes."

His were nearly black, atavistic. And yet he smiled. A wicked, satisfied smile. Perhaps even conspiratorial, as though he saw something similar in the windows to her soul that was alive in him.

In that second, she had no defenses against him at all. Not physically or emotionally. She felt intensely vulnerable as he pressed, stretching and filling her until they were locked together. Her knees reflexively bent to hug his hips, somehow making him sink even more flush against her, settling deep within her.

She hadn't realized that sex was so raw. So deliberate. It struck her that she had met him mere days ago, but it was a startling moment of alignment. Of sharing an experience.

"Hurt?" he murmured.

She barely heard and barely comprehended. She was lost to the magnitude of the moment. She couldn't keep her eyes open as waves of emotion washed over her. There was a sweet sense of achievement and the stinging discomfort of uncertainty. But there was also a tender yearning that closed her limbs around him, needing the reassurance of his hot body tight against hers.

"When you're ready," he said against her ear. He kissed across her jaw and temple, the pressure light and frustratingly elusive.

Before she consciously knew what she wanted or what she was signaling, her body shifted restlessly beneath his. Her inner muscles clenched, and the golden light from the lamp seemed to fill her. Possibility arrived within her, stoking a slippery heat in her loins, filling her with renewed hunger and yearning.

"Yes," he hissed. "Exactly like that." He licked into the delicate hollow beneath her ear.

As he withdrew, everything in her clenched to hold on to him.

He cupped the side of her neck so she felt the pressure of his strong palm against her throbbing artery. She didn't know which was hotter, his skin or hers.

He returned, flooding her with such a wave of pleasurable sensations, she groaned. The arousal that had been banked while she adjusted to this new act spun through her, catching at her with its tendrils, dragging her back into the sharp tumble of acute desire.

He thrust again, and she felt the strain in his back against her palms as she roamed her touch, urging him on. He kept the pace slow, giving her time to adjust, but her body knew what it wanted. The next time he returned, her hips tilted in greeting. Her thighs clenched on his hips, fighting his next withdrawal, making him hiss in a combination of pleasured excitement and disciplined exertion.

She slid her hands to his lower back and lower still, digging her fingernails into his buttocks to drive him into her with more power.

He began to move faster, setting her afire.

Their skin dampened with perspiration. They kissed and kissed again, catching at each other's lips while groaning in an earthly mingle of noises. Her reactions were pure instinct. She arched and pressed her tongue into his mouth, locked her calf across his backside and made noises of agony.

With each thrust she lost a little more of herself, but she threw herself willingly into their erotic struggle. Their fight to reach completion together. Her climax approached, and he grew more ardent, as if he sensed it. Her entire world narrowed to the destination they sought, and suddenly it was there, vast and full of endless possibility.

For one heartbeat, she thought the way he stiffened meant he was in paradise without her. Then a profound, crashing wave engulfed her. After that, she didn't know which of them trembled or shook, which pulsed or contracted, only that they were in this maelstrom together. Thrown and tossed, battered and exalted. Both equally, utterly, gloriously destroyed.

CHAPTER EIGHT

As Rhys dragged free of her, the final caressing stroke on his sensitized skin was pure, velvety bliss that jangled against his nerve endings. He landed on his damp back, the blankets tangled beneath him, and listened to Sopi take a full breath and release it as a hum of supreme satisfaction.

He lay motionless, a castaway barely alive on a remote island beach. The storm had left him weak and boneless, fighting to catch his breath.

Beside him, Sopi was still panting. Her damp arm was against his. Somehow their hands found each other, and their fingers entwined in a silent reassurance that they had made it through to live another day.

Warning signals crept through the fog of his recovery, though. He had somehow managed to keep enough wits about him to be gentle and ensure her pleasure, but he had been completely abandoned to their lovemaking. Lost to a pleasure that was even more exquisite and profound than he'd anticipated. Addictive, even.

It was the novelty of being naked without protection, he assured himself, even as his hand tightened on hers, wanting to draw her deeper into his protective sphere. He closed his eyes and fought the sense of a rising force within him that wanted to somehow bind her to him.

He should have realized her effect on him was dangerously intense when he'd tracked her like a damned arctic wolf following the scent of his mate into the snow. With the clarity of hindsight, he saw how he'd leaped on the convenience of her royal blood so he could have this—her naked body beside his own.

Now they'd embarked on the making of a child. The reality of that hit him like a meteor from space, crashing emotions over him—responsibility, concern, pride, excitement and a fear of the unknown. Terror of the uncontrollable.

He threw his free arm across his eyes, hand

knotting into a fist as he tried to stave off the maelstrom of conflict. If he reacted this powerfully to the mere possibility of making a child, how would he cope if they'd actually made one?

He had put himself in an impossible position, he realized, and there was no way to change it now.

"Thank you," Sopi murmured, stirring beside him. She rolled and bent her knee so her soft thigh settled on his. Her head turned into his shoulder, and her damp lips pressed against his skin.

His nerve endings leaped and the spent flesh between his thighs pulsed with a fresh rush of heat. The compulsion to gather her up and roll atop her and consume her all over again was nearly more than he could withstand.

This was impossible.

Intolerable.

But he couldn't push her away, dewy virgin that she was. He might hate himself for giving in to his desire for her, but he would hate himself even more if he hurt her.

He lifted his arm from between them and

opened his legs so her knee fell between his own, cuddling her into his side.

"*How* was a woman with that much passion still a virgin?" he asked in a voice graveled by satisfaction.

"I was saving it all for you, obviously." Her fingertips drew a lazy circle across his abdomen.

His heart gave a rolling pound of thrill at the thought. He was too rational and forward-thinking to put virginity on a pedestal, but there was something deeply satisfying in the sense of promise in her words.

He was in so much trouble.

"Was it…okay for you?" she asked tentatively.

He groaned and caught her teasing hand. "It was exquisite. You are." He brought her hand to his mouth so he could lightly bite her fingers. "But you should probably go to sleep before I start thinking we should double-check whether it was really that incredible."

She hummed a sensual noise of amusement and moved against him restlessly, drying his throat. "How can I sleep if there's any question in our minds?"

He was still at war with his elemental self, but the primitive won again. He promised himself he would withhold more of himself this time and pulled her atop him.

Her hair spilled around him, and he was lost.

Sopi wasn't so inexperienced that she believed falling in love two weeks into a relationship was a realistic expectation. Even so, she was quite sure she was on her way. Rhys was such a remarkable man!

The more she learned of Verina's history and how hard he had struggled to return to their homeland, the more she admired him for all he had accomplished. He was earnest in his support of his charities and keen to develop green initiatives. He had a dry wit and a sharp intelligence, and he genuinely cared what happened to his country and the world.

When they were in public, he gave her room to find her way while remaining a steady presence, always backing her up when she was unsure. In private, he offered romantic gestures like touching a rose to her chin or putting a ring on her finger while they stood on the palace wall overlooking the lake.

And then there were the nights, the magnificent nights when they couldn't seem to quench their insatiable passion for each other.

How could she not fall for a man who did all those things to her and for her and...

She counted the days again, heart tripping over itself and tripping up her brain.

She was only a day late, nothing to get excited about. A lot had happened lately. She was handling the move to Verina and her new title and all the public attention fairly well, but this was a huge deal. It could easily be throwing off her cycle. She was often late when she was stressed. She certainly didn't feel any different. No nausea or sore breasts, which she knew from friends were very typical signs.

Even so, her hand went to her abdomen and her eyes closed over emotive tears. She bit her smile, trying to keep the beams of happiness from bursting out of her like balls of sunlight.

This had to be love she was experiencing. Why else would she be this elated at the idea of being pregnant? Obviously, love for her child was taking root in her, but a baby was pure wishful thinking at this point. No, this was more. This was a certainty that she wanted Rhys's baby.

Because she loved him.

She waited a few more days before she said anything to him, not wanting to get his hopes up. They were dressing for their official engagement ball in Paris. It seemed a bit overkill when they were marrying in a month, but the party covered the fact that Henrik had come to a Paris clinic for surgery.

When their maids and valets and assistants left them alone, she clutched her hands before her and watched Rhys check his bow tie in the mirror. He turned and tracked a gaze rich with admiration over every inch of her.

"You're stunning."

"I'm late."

He flicked his glance to the clock. "Fashionably. We're the guests of honor. It's expected," he dismissed.

"No, I mean..." She nearly ruined her lipstick, biting back her smile at the way he'd misinterpreted her.

He actually swayed backward as comprehension struck. "Late," he repeated blankly. "Are you...sure?"

He wasn't smiling, and her own smile faltered.

"I'm sure I'm late. I'm not sure of...anything else. Sometimes I'm off if I have a lot going on in my life." She hitched a shoulder, reminding herself that she didn't want to mislead him, but she had rather hoped for more excitement. "I'll...um...make a doctor's appointment when we get back to Verina, but I thought you'd want to know."

She started to move forward into his arms. In the last days, they'd become quite comfortable in offering affection when they were alone, but something in his demeanor made her falter.

"Are you...not pleased?"

"No, of course I am," he assured her. "But if it hasn't been confirmed..."

She nodded, cheeks feeling skinned. In her mind, this conversation was supposed to swirl with excitement and laughter. Her tentative words of love had been on the tip of her tongue. Now her emotions were crashing into each other like a ten-car pileup.

"I don't mean to be lukewarm." He caught her by the elbows and brushed his lips against her cheek. "This is exactly what we want, but Elise had a lot of disappointments. Let's wait to be sure before we celebrate."

Was that really what was going on? She searched his expression, but he avoided her gaze, moving to open the door. He offered his arm again.

"We should go. I want Henrik to be able to leave the party as soon as possible if he needs to."

Rhys kept his emotions firmly locked down, fearful of letting one out lest they all spill. There was a part of him wanting to scream with pride and excitement, but no. It wasn't even confirmed yet, and a thousand things could still go wrong. There could be medical implications for Sopi. Why had he not thought of that before they'd had unprotected sex? How irresponsible of him.

Then there was the guilt, wider and darker and deeper than any of those other emotions, especially when he looked into his brother's eyes and accepted Henrik's congratulatory handshake on his official engagement.

Henrik's words had been a public expression of his approval that Sopi was joining their family, but Rhys felt like a traitor, holding the secret of his potential heir in the shadows of his heart.

Now Henrik was beside him in a more informal capacity.

"You're right," Henrik said, watching Sopi. "She's more than she seems. You chose well."

Rhys couldn't argue. Sopi was fully embracing the woman she had been meant to become. She wore an elegant, one-shouldered gown in champagne silk with sparkling beadwork scrolling around her waist. Her hair was in a knot and adorned with sparkling pins. If Rhys stared at it too long, he began thinking of the silky feel of it slithering across his stomach and thighs—a distraction he couldn't afford.

He dragged his attention from where Elise was introducing Sopi to a founder of a charity and met his brother's shrewdly assessing gaze.

Henrik had stood to toast them and had

been the first to cut in when Rhys had started the dancing with Sopi. Henrik had since danced with his wife and made the rounds to speak with guests, but he was pale. Rhys thought he should call it a night.

"You're both quite convincing," Henrik said.

"In what way?"

"That you're in love."

"That's the point," Rhys said, grimly aware that the infatuation he was displaying wasn't nearly as manufactured as he had planned it to be. When he wasn't fantasizing about having sex with Sopi, he was telling Gerard to check in with her, to ensure she didn't need him. Or he was trolling social media, ensuring no one was saying anything that might impact her growing self-confidence.

Meanwhile, she was taking on palace duties and public appearances like a pro, earning goodwill wherever she went. The one time she had prevailed on him for his opinion, she had just received Francine's report on Cassiopeia's. She had wanted him to confirm her instincts, worried she was too invested to be objective. She wasn't.

In every way, she was rising to the challenge of her station. He couldn't be prouder. Now she was likely fulfilling their most important duty, and he didn't know how to handle how vulnerable it made him feel. How guilty.

"Elise is convinced Sopi's in love with you," Henrik commented.

Rhys yanked his attention back to his brother. When their gazes clashed again, his brother's held rebuke.

"I can't control how she feels." And there, too, he was at war with himself. In every way, he wanted to pull her in, hold her tight, but there was that clear-thinking part of him that saw the peril in it.

"Do you return those feelings?"

"Read my diary and find out." They had long ago perfected their ability to speak about private subjects in public and express annoyance with each other without it being readable on their faces. "Why would you ask me something like that? Here?"

"At your engagement party?"

"I don't interfere in your relationship with

Elise. Kindly show me the same consideration."

Henrik laughed outright. "We're not counting the three years you badgered me to propose to her?"

"You were miserable. I was concerned about mankind as a whole."

"I was giving her a choice. I didn't know what my future would look like. Would I regain the throne and make her a queen? Lose all those investment gambles we were taking and force her to live in a shack? I didn't know if they would *accept* her. I loved her too much to start our life together on a string of false promises."

"I haven't made any false promises to Sopi."

"Haven't you? As I said, you're very convincing. If you're not *actually* in love…"

Rhys muttered a curse under his breath. "I care about her. Of course I do."

"She more than cares, Rhys. She's putting her heart into this. Into *you*."

He knew that. If she was carrying his child, she was so deeply invested, he couldn't quantify it.

And even though Sopi wasn't a needy person, she did have needs. He had promised to be her anchor and foundation and sounding board, which he was. He couldn't take many steps back from that, but he refused to take further emotional ones forward.

The resulting conflict was both a sense of walls closing in and a rack of tension, pulling him toward a breaking point.

"I would prefer you focus on yourself and your own wife," Rhys said. "I'll worry about Sopi."

"I have never understood your desire to close yourself off this way. What is the worst that could happen, Rhys? Elise is my source of strength. Let Sopi become that for you."

His brother could die. That was the worst that could happen. And the helplessness he felt at the prospect of that was more than he could bear. How was Sopi supposed to help him through such a thing? He wouldn't put that sort of burden on her.

No, he had to maintain what was left of his reserve for all their sakes.

Sopi somehow kept a smile on her face, but she kept looking to Rhys, anxious that his reaction to her possible pregnancy had been so tepid.

He was locked in a discussion with Henrik. Elise was right. The two were very close. Sopi was both envious and jealous, having always wished for a sibling, especially one she could confide in the way the men seemed to confide in each other.

She was also a teensy bit threatened by their closeness. Elise had found her place in that dynamic a long time ago. She knew how to pry her way between them and where her marriage took precedence over the fealty between the brothers, but Sopi came up against it like a force field.

Until this evening, she had thought that was the source of this distance she sensed between them. An inequality of sorts. Tonight, she had seen the true problem. She might be in love, but Rhys wasn't.

Which turned her engagement party into a nightmare.

The chatty woman monopolizing her finally took a breath. Sopi was able to say, "Will you excuse me? I need to visit the powder room."

On her way down the hall, she veered onto a balcony for a moment to herself. Her arrival interrupted a couple who broke apart with a stammer and a blush before hurrying away. Their clinch had been tame, but their deep embarrassment meant it had been a very private moment. That left Sopi agonizing for a similar emotional connection with Rhys.

Oh, irony, you devil. Initially, she had balked at marrying him, worried this fairy-tale world she'd risen to would be more than she could handle. Now she wanted the whole package. The declaration of love and the happily-ever-after.

It would come with time, she tried telling herself, trying not to cry. Other things were settling into place. Her friendship with Elise was growing by the day, and even she and Henrik shared a laugh now and again. The job of being a princess wasn't proving too onerous. She looked forward to being a mother.

No, this was old-fashioned bridal nerves, maybe even hormonal changes making her feel like she needed more from Rhys.

As she blinked to clear the blurred vision of

the Eiffel Tower, a sixth sense made the hairs stand up on the back of her neck. The door clicked behind her and there was a scuffed footstep.

"Well, well, well."

The voice might as well have been a knife blade tracing down her spine. Sopi's back went tense and rail straight. She fought the urge to clench her fists as a hot-cold flush of angry dread washed over her.

She knew instantly who the voice belonged to and stole a brief second to erase any traces of despondency from her expression. In the busy days since she had left Canada, she had only fleetingly thought of her stepmother and stepsisters. Francine had mentioned their names in relation to some unpaid invoices, but otherwise, Sopi had not missed any of them one bit.

With a fresh layer of composure in place, she turned and faced Nanette.

Her stepsister wore a striking black gown that plunged down the front to her belly button. The frothy chiffon skirt had a slit to the top of her thigh. She wore gold evening shoes peppered in bling and her bloodred lipstick

matched her nails. Her lips parted in a malev-
olent smile as she approached with the slink
of a stalking cat. Or a slithering snake.

"Fancy meeting you here."

"I didn't know you were invited," Sopi
said. If she had, she might have taken steps
to change that. She wasn't feeling hostile or
vengeful toward her stepfamily, but neither
was she eager to speak to any of them again.

"I'm insulted you didn't make a point of
inviting us. I had to come as a plus one. But
I suppose you can't be expected to grasp the
finer points of etiquette, given your rustic
upbringing."

Sopi had precious seconds to weigh her options. Making a scene was not one of them,
but she couldn't allow Nanette to intimidate
her. The little bit of confidence she had developed in recent weeks had already been battered by the knowledge Rhys wasn't falling
in love with her the way she was falling for
him. But her self-worth was too hard-won for
her to let this confrontation knock her flat.
Rhys would be disappointed in her if she let
Nanette get the better of her, and she would
be disappointed in herself.

Which left her taking a similar approach to her old one. She kept the peace by grasping at patience and speaking politely while trying to project the sophistication she was desperately trying to develop.

"It's lovely to see you again either way," she lied. "Where are you making your home now?"

Nanette laughed, but it was the patronizing chuckle of a superior amused by the antics of a lesser creature. "Full marks for *that*."

Sopi didn't let herself be drawn into whatever crass reaction Nanette was trying to provoke. "Your mother and sister are well?" she persevered.

"Oh, we're really doing this? Yes, Mummy leased us a bleak little walk-up in Vienna because she had to take what she could get on short notice. Fernanda and I would prefer to be here in Paris. You might have mentioned the royal bloodline." She narrowed her eyes with malevolence.

"I'm surprised your mother never unearthed it. She's always found my family to be so enriching." Okay, now she was descending to Nanette's level. She glanced to the glass doorway back to the hallway, noting the shift of one of the bodyguards against the glass. She signaled that she was fine and he should let her handle this.

"Well, look who finally grew a pair," Nanette said after a beat of astonishment.

Sopi realized her hands had closed into fists and consciously loosened them. She and Nanette both wore heels, but the other woman was taller. Sopi had to lift her chin to look down her nose at her.

"Someone told me once that I should set standards for myself and not drop below them," Sopi said with a meaningless smile. "This conversation is one of those things plummeting past acceptable. Excuse me."

"Oh, is acknowledging your stepsister beneath you? Now that you have a title and a presumably concussed fiancé?"

"Of course not," Sopi lied, even though alarm streaked through her veins. "You've taken *so many* pains over the years to tell me that you're far too well-bred to behave in a crass manner."

"It's not crass to pay back a double cross," Nanette shot back. "It's survival."

"You're accusing *me* of a double cross?" Sopi choked on a ball of outrage. "You sold my home behind my back!"

"Is that what happened? Because this whole thing feels like a setup. How did you even know him?"

"I didn't."

"You must have," Nanette snapped, growing genuinely angry. "How did he even find out who you were? Is it even real? I can't believe he actually wants you, title or not. Do you have money? Does he need it?"

"That's enough." A hot flush of temper stung her cheeks. "Stop before this turns ugly."

"Ugly is throwing people out into the snow at *midnight*."

"I didn't ask that you be treated that way." Was she sorry? Probably not as much as she should be.

"You took control of the hotel that night. Of course that order came from *you*, you hideous bitch."

Don't engage, Sopi told herself. Through the windows, she saw another shift of light, but she was determined to handle this herself.

"I didn't order it," she insisted, but she was piqued enough to bite back. "The timing of your departure was always your choice, Nanette. You could have left long ago. Months. *Years*, in fact."

"Oh, does the student think she's becoming the master?" Nanette asked with a hoot of astonishment. "Allow me to demonstrate how much you still have to learn, Sopi. Start compensating me for the insults you've delivered or I will go straight back into that ballroom and tell everyone you're a janitor with a side hustle that looks like brothel work. No one believes you're in *love*," she dismissed scathingly. "You obviously compromised him in some way and now you're blackmailing him."

"*Who* is resorting to blackmail?"

Nanette tilted her head and smiled with false charm. "Make it worth my while to keep my mouth shut or I will."

Sopi moved closer, driven by old anger and new hurt and feelings that were so fresh and raw, she hadn't processed them, but she damned sure wasn't going to be walked on by this harridan ever again. And she wouldn't let Nanette harm Rhys to get at her, either.

"Think about what you're doing, Nanette," she warned in a voice that originated in a grim place behind her heart. She had to tilt back her head and her body was quivering in reaction, but a frightening thrust of power emboldened her. "Look at who I am now. You do *not* want to start a war with me."

"I know exactly who you are. You're a joke, Sopi."

"My name is Cassiopeia." She leaned in. "But *you* can call me Your Highness."

Nanette struck like a viper with a slap that snapped Sopi's head to the side. She was so stunned, she stumbled back a few steps, hardly able to make sense of the fact that she'd been struck, let alone retaliate.

The door behind her crashed open. There was a blur of movement as Rhys took hold of Nanette and thrust her toward a bodyguard.

"Get her out of here. Have her arrested for assault."

"What? You can't do that to me!" Nanette's screech of protest and furious struggle halted when the bodyguard mentioned handcuffs. With one hate-filled glare, she let the burly man escort her from the balcony.

"Are you hurt?" Rhys positioned himself to block any view of her from the windows.

"I think so." She ran her tongue in the space between her teeth and cheek and tasted copper. Beneath her testing fingers, her jaw was scorching hot.

She was shaking, though, and stepped closer to him, expecting him to pull her into his arms.

He only shifted to settle one tense arm around her. "We should get ice on that. Let's go upstairs."

"What are people going to think if we leave? Did anyone see?"

"I'll issue a statement. Don't worry about it."

He looked so incensed, her stomach flipped with apprehension. He moved to hold the door for her.

Thankfully, the balcony was right off the hallway to the elevators and powder room. They only had to cross to where one of his bodyguards was already waiting with an open car. A handful of people glanced and murmured with speculation, but within seconds they were silently traveling up to their suite.

"I'm really sorry," she whispered, heart thudding at his granite profile. "I didn't mean for anything like this to happen. I didn't even know she was here."

He looked to the guard. "Find out who brought her. Blackball him."

The man nodded and touched his ear to repeat the instruction to someone else.

"Rhys." She set a hand on his arm. He was like iron. Marble. The sort of rough diamonds that came out of the earth flawed and hard and only good for drilling into rock. "I don't think whoever brought her is to blame."

"He lied to get her past security. If I'd seen her name on the list, I would have had them turned away."

They arrived in their suite, and he barked at her assistant to get an ice pack.

Wide-eyed, the young woman complied, hurrying back with a compress wrapped in a hand towel. "Should I call a doctor?"

"I'm fine," Sopi insisted.

"Write down these names." Rhys recited Sopi's stepfamily. "I want alerts on all of them. Reports. Where they live, who they're seeing. Financials. Any pressure points. Tell Gerard I want my lawyer and PR on the phone as quickly as possible."

"Yes, sir." She hurried away, leaving them alone.

"I don't think she came here planning to hit me. I provoked her," Sopi admitted miserably. "I should have walked away instead of letting her get under my skin. It was my first chance to push back after all these years and I..." She'd been upset over *him* and his reaction to her news. She had taken it out on Nanette. "I told her to call me..." She cringed. "Your Highness."

"She should. It's who you are," he asserted coldly.

She shook her head. "No, I was stooping to her level. This is my fault—"

"The hell it is." She had never seen him so hardhearted. "Has she hit you before? You should have told me."

"No! Never. I didn't imagine she was capable of it. That's why I waved off the bodyguard. But I really don't think she'll do anything like it again. You're overreacting."

"I am *not*," he hurled at her. "This sort of thing gets quashed at the larva stage." He pointed at the floor. "Otherwise it grows into a goddamned siege."

Oh. She started to understand what was driving his pitiless rage. She sank onto the sofa and lowered the ice from her face. "Can we please talk this out?" she asked tentatively.

"There's nothing to talk out. I'm doing what has to be done. We won't go downstairs again. You can undress, have a bath, make yourself comfortable, but keep that ice on your face." His gaze bounced off the spot that was probably hued red by the ice. "I shouldn't have left you alone. I thought you were going to the ladies' room." He flinched with self-recrimination before his expression hardened. "It won't happen again."

"Rhys, this isn't your fault."

Something in the way he gathered himself told her he was traveling inward to a place that wasn't reachable. Not right now anyway. Not by her.

"A bath sounds nice," she murmured, wanting some time alone herself. "Call me if you need me."

* * *

Sopi woke hours later and realized Rhys hadn't come to bed.

Puzzled, she went in search and found him in the guest room.

"I didn't want to disturb you," he said when she hovered in the door. "You should get your rest."

"It's nothing, Rhys. I'm totally fine." A faint red mark, but nothing a sweep of makeup wouldn't hide. She crossed to lift the covers and join him.

He caught them, stopping her. "What are you doing?"

"I want to sleep with you." She released the blankets and crossed her arms to catch up her nightgown, smoothly skimming it up and over her head. She dropped it to the floor and stood nude in the moonlight.

"I'm not at my best, Sopi."

She had noticed, and she didn't know how to change that except to get close to him physically.

She lowered to sit on the bed, hip aligned to his, and began unraveling the hair she had braided before she went to bed. She did it slowly, in the sort of tease he usually enjoyed.

"I'm not in the mood to play." He spoke through his teeth, catching at her hands to stop her. "I'm too wound up."

"Then you need to relax." She shifted to brace her hands on his shoulders, leaning over him. "Want a massage?" That always turned into lovemaking, but that's where she was aiming. She desperately needed to reconnect with him and assure herself they were still okay. Was this about her possibly being pregnant? About Nanette? Or was it something deeper? Something she had done?

She didn't land the kiss she went seeking. In one lithe movement, he had her on her back and loomed over her.

"You shouldn't be in here, Sopi. I don't have a good grip on myself."

"You sound like a werewolf. I'm not *afraid* of you," she said with a small laugh, petting his beard but catching enough to give a gentle tug. "You would never hurt me. I know that." She slid her hand to the back of his head, inviting him to kiss her.

"No, but—" His fingers dug into her shoulders, and his neck muscles bunched in refusal. He really did need a massage. He was gripped by something rigid and painful and clearly needed release.

She lifted her head to press her mouth to his.

With an animalistic groan, he pressed her flat beneath him and raked his lips across her own.

It wasn't the gentle seduction she was used to. It was raw need. A quest to drag her into some dark place he already occupied. As she moved with greeting beneath him, trying to settle into a more comfortable position, she could feel through the blankets that he was already aroused. He hardened his arms around her, keeping her in place as he scraped his teeth down her neck. His mouth opened in damp suction against her skin before his hand took possession of her breast, plumping it for plundering.

When he sucked, pleasure streaked like golden lightning from her nipple to her loins. They normally built up to this sort of intensity. His boldness threw her into an electrical storm, but she gloried in the wildness of it. This wasn't the civilized man she knew, but she recognized him in a far more primitive way. Her mate.

She grasped at his straining shoulders and back, encouraging him to keep ravaging her. She grew a little rough herself, catching a fist in his hair and dragging him up to kiss her. She stabbed her tongue into his mouth.

He didn't let her become the aggressor. He cupped her jaw and took her mouth with blatant eroticism until she was limp beneath him, pulsing all over with anticipation.

Then, with a noise like a wounded animal, he yanked the blankets from between them. One of his strong arms hooked under her leg, hiking it high so she was utterly helpless as he guided his turgid shape against her wet folds, moving easily in the gathered moisture, stoking the ache and strumming chords of pleasure through her.

"Stop me," he commanded, the crest of his sex demanding access.

She shook her head, too caught up in her own craven need. "Do it," she urged.

With a guttural sound, he thrust, driving easily into her slippery depths. As he came flush against her, he gave an extra pulse of his hips to ensure he was firmly seated inside her.

She had never experienced anything so earthy before. So primeval. He smothered her with a kiss, and when she bent her free knee, he gathered that one on his other arm and knelt to brace above her, pinning her with her legs open as he withdrew and thrust, watching her.

She was surrounded by him. Claimed by him and willing to be whatever he needed in this moment. She lost herself in the pools of his blue eyes as he undulated with power and purpose. She wanted to lift to kiss him, but her hair was pinned under her back, holding her head against the mattress. The restraint added an erotic twist to their coupling. She couldn't move except to caress damp skin stretched taut over hard muscles and sinew and bones.

And she couldn't escape the pleasure he relentlessly wound tight inside her. She grew sweaty and so acutely aroused, she couldn't stand it.

"Rhys," she sobbed.

He shifted, tucked his hands beneath her cheeks to tilt her hips. The new angle meant fresh nerve endings took his next thrust. Lust surged in her. Something pure and sharp and splendid.

He dropped his head to taste her lips, and she licked between his own with utter abandon, submerged in a hot pool of lava, thick and melting and incendiary.

She urged him to keep going, never let this stop, but she couldn't withstand this intensity. Just when she thought she would burst into flames, the world exploded around her.

He plunged deep and stayed there, pulsing hard within her as she twisted in the throes of her own unbearable pleasure, both of them groaning in carnal ecstasy.

Drained, Rhys realized he was crushing Sopi and forced his still twitching muscles to shift him off her.

He had known he was at his worst when he had finished making statements and recalibrating their security. He'd taken a cold shower to cool his temper, but he'd still been too edgy to sleep. He had wanted sex, but

Sopi had been asleep, and he had known his mood wasn't gentle. He'd made himself come to this other bed and had been lying here aching with arousal, seriously reconsidering whether they should marry after all, given the way he was reacting.

When he'd heard her moving through the suite, the beast in him had nearly howled for her.

And she had arrived as though in answer, stripped naked and offered herself.

Such a fight he'd put up, too. He'd taken her with all the finesse of a rutting boar. What if she was pregnant?

With his gut aching, he asked with dread, "Did I hurt you?"

"Of course not," she chided, rolling toward him.

"I was rough." He didn't let her touch him, not trusting himself to stay off her. He sat up on the side of the bed.

"Rhys." She came up behind him, knees bracketing his hips. She wrapped her arms around his shoulders so her breasts pressed into his back. Her scent was all around him, almost impossible to resist in its inducement to turn and take her in his arms, especially when she said, "We've been vigorous before. It was exciting."

It had been a snap of something inside him.

He had been lying here berating himself for hesitating at the door to the balcony. He had wanted to give Sopi the chance to assert herself with her stepsister, but the sudden flash of Nanette's swiping hand had nearly turned him homicidal. It had been all he could do to stay this side of civilized and leave Nanette to the authorities.

His feelings for Sopi were becoming way more than he could handle. He couldn't let her go, though. What if she was already pregnant?

She nipped at his shoulder and rubbed her lips to soothe, fanning all his basest instincts. "I would have told you if you were hurting me. Honestly? I liked that you let go for once. You made me feel sexy and desired. Needed." Her voice held a throb. She was a bright woman. She knew he was holding back from her emotionally.

Much as he hated himself for hurting her,

he stood to confront her, trying to cement the barriers in place for both of them.

"My losing control isn't a good thing, Sopi."

Even in the dim light he saw the flash of injury in her expression. He heard it in her voice.

"It wasn't *bad*," she argued, but he heard her quaver of uncertainty. "It means we're at a place in our relationship where we can get a little wild and still have full trust. You wanted me to trust you, and I do."

"You might be pregnant!" He paced away, hand going into his hair and giving a yank of frustration.

"For heaven's sake, you weren't *violent*. We just got to the good part a lot faster than usual."

"I was still crude as hell."

"It was uninhibited. Passionate. It was love-making at its finest. Literally *love*making. For me, at least," she added with a hesitant lilt in her tone.

"Don't," he commanded, naked and cold in the shaft of blue light from the window. "Don't fall in love with me, Sopi."

"Why not?" she cried in a flash of angry pain that left a mark on his heart.

"Because I can't fall in love with you." And he couldn't stay here and watch her eyes fill with tears like that. "You can sleep here. I'll go to the other bed."

He left before he couldn't.

CHAPTER NINE

SOPI MOVED THROUGH the next minutes and hours and days in a type of shell shock. Rhys didn't love her, didn't want to love her and refused to talk about it.

She made a doctor's appointment for later in the week, now equally as anxious as she was excited by the idea of being pregnant. She distracted herself by staying on top of things at the palace and making appearances with Rhys and having a fitting for her wedding dress—which should have been one of the happiest things she'd ever done, but it was all she could do to hold back sobs of wretchedness.

In public, she and Rhys continued to play the part of devoted lovers, but they were sleeping apart and barely speaking except in stilted bursts. A few times she caught a look of deep regret on his face, but she always looked away and shored up her own defenses, too hurt by his rejection to bear his remorse over breaking her heart.

She should probably regret all of this. A pregnancy would tie her to a man who didn't love her, but the truth was, she *deeply* wanted to be pregnant. Maybe it wasn't the best circumstances, but since leaving Canada, she'd been feeling very rootless. She needed family. She knew that now. A baby would give her the deep connection to another human being that Rhys was so reluctant to provide.

Which was why she was so devastated to get her period while she was dressing for her doctor's appointment.

Reeling in anguish, she tried to dismiss the maid who entered. "Can you leave me alone, please?" she said, trying to stifle the rush of tears.

"Yes, but the prince said when you're ready, he's in the lounge..." She curtsied and hurried away.

Rhys had arranged to take her to the appointment himself. She allowed herself one silent scream into a wet facecloth, then blew her nose and repaired her makeup.

Bracing herself, she walked into the lounge. Found a distant smile for Gerard.

"Will you please cancel my appointment and give us the room?" she asked him.

"Of course." He sent a brief glance of surprise between her and Rhys's arrested expression, then made himself scarce.

Rhys was headed to a meeting after the appointment. He wore a suit and tie. It fitted him as beautifully as every other piece of clothing he owned, but she thought he looked gaunt.

For the first time in days, his shields seemed to thin as he searched her expression. "What's wrong?"

Besides everything? She didn't know how they had gone from so great to so terrible in less than a week, but telling him she might be pregnant seemed to have been the instigator. Was she supposed to be happy that was no longer an issue?

"I'm not pregnant," she announced through a tight throat.

A flash of something that might have been agony streaked across his features, and he rocked on his heels, nudged off his keel for the first time since the night of their engagement party.

He quickly schooled his expression into something more cautious. "A miscarriage?"

"I told you I might just be late," she said defensively. "It happens when I'm stressed." But even as she dismissed it as no real loss, her heart hit rock bottom. She waited in vain for a hug and some expression of sorrow that came anywhere near to the devastation wrapping itself around her.

She heard him draw breath to say something, but he seemed to change his mind at the last second. She heard it anyway.

Next time.

Her cramping middle knotted even more. She stood paralyzed by torment as the full scope of what she'd done began to hit her. She had agreed to marry him. To sleep with him until she had his babies. Plural. And she would do that while knowing he would never love her. Then she would have to make a life with him and their children.

While he wore a look of such regret, she felt sick.

Her eyes brimmed until she couldn't see him through her curtain of misery.

"We can try again, but not tonight," she choked. "There's no point. I'll tell you when I'm…" Fertile? Receptive? "Able."

"Sopi," he said to her back, but she closed her door. Shut him out as neatly as he'd been shutting her out.

He leaned his hands on the back of the sofa and breathed through the fiery agony that gripped him. This was why he didn't want to fall in love with her. The baby hadn't even been real yet. He hadn't allowed himself to believe she was pregnant, trying to wait until the doctor had confirmed it before he let himself get attached to the idea of being a father, yet he was as devastated as if she'd been months along and he'd already felt the damned thing move.

In his helplessness, he had searched desperately for words that might wipe that anguished expression from her face, knowing a platitude about trying again wouldn't cut it.

She'd heard it anyway and shut him down. *I'll tell you when I'm able.*

He ran his hand down his face, aching to make love to her again. Not to conceive, but to feel her. Hold her and smell her hair and say nonsense things across the pillow.

Henrik was wrong. He hadn't chosen well. He had chosen selfishly. Yes, she ticked all the boxes. A thousand women could have done that. He had allowed his baser instincts to guide him, though. He had given in to the primeval part of himself, manipulated her into their engagement only to cause her all this pain.

He went through the motions of his day, and when he returned to the palace, he ate alone, brooding, trying to see how they could forge a way forward.

He woke to the disturbing news that his brother and Elise were returning within the hour from Paris and wanted to see him the moment they arrived.

Throat dry and appetite nonexistent, he nearly fell over when Sopi hurried into the breakfast room, an anxious look on her face. She wore a jacket with a straight skirt since she was due at a school later today. Her hair was in a rope-twist ponytail, her makeup light.

"Why are they coming back in the middle of his treatment?" she asked, voice thick with apprehension.

"I don't know." He didn't like any of the possible answers.

Whatever she read in his expression had her crossing to him and pushing her cool hand into his stiff one.

"I won't stay if they don't want me there, but I'll come to their room with you."

He should have said it was unnecessary. He was a big boy, but it was all he could do not to crush her slender fingers. He kept her hand in his until word came that his brother had arrived. Then he drew Sopi with him down the gallery to the monarch's wing.

His throat was full of gravel, his chest nothing but broken glass. Thank God for Sopi, because she found a warm smile for her soon-to-be in-laws as they were shown into the private parlor where Henrik was seated. He looked gray. Elise stood beside him, clasping his hand. They were both beaming.

"Oh," Sopi breathed in relief. "We thought

you were staying in Paris for the entire course of your treatment. Is everything going well?"

"As well as can be expected," Henrik said with a dismissive flick of his hand. "I toss more than I eat, but the doctors aren't too concerned. I have a three-day break now, and we missed sleeping in our own bed. Plus, we had news we couldn't wait to share." He looked up at his wife.

Elise was blinking tearful eyes at him.

"We're pregnant," Henrik said.

The announcement hit Rhys like a shock wave. Distantly, he heard Sopi's breath rush out as though she'd been punched. He recovered first, probably because he was used to staying on his feet through life's groin kicks. He wanted to hold on to Sopi's hand, somehow protect her from what she must be feeling, but she pulled her hand free of his.

He was genuinely happy for the pair, though. They'd waited so long for this.

"That's amazing." He moved to kiss Elise's cheeks. "No one deserves such good news more. Congratulations." He shook his brother's hand, unable to hide his astonishment.

"We're as shocked as you are," Elise said as she accepted the shaky embrace Sopi offered.

Only Rhys detected how pale Sopi was and how unsteady her smile was.

"We had completely given up trying after my diagnosis," Henrik said. "But we had a last hurrah before my surgery." He winked.

"Henrik!" Elise nudged his shoulder, blushing and laughing. "That's untoward."

"It's a miracle." He caught her hand again and kissed it. "We won't be making any formal announcements, but we wanted you both to know. I've put a lot on your shoulders lately and we have discovered how counterproductive that sort of pressure can be. Better to…how shall I say? Celebrate what you have rather than pin your heart to an uncertain future."

"But never give up hope, either," Elise hurried to add.

"No, you never do, do you?" Henrik said to her with an emotive look at his wife. "How did I ever get so lucky?"

"We'll leave you to rest," Rhys said mechanically as all the implications of this news began to penetrate his skull.

* * *

Sopi walked in a daze back to their wing, unaware whether Rhys had offered his arm or not. She was too encased in throes of envy. She was genuinely pleased for them, of course, especially now she'd had a taste of how disappointing it was to fail to conceive. Even so, she had to press the tremble of anguish from her lips.

"That opens up fresh possibilities, doesn't it?" Rhys asked as he closed the door to their lounge in what sounded like an ominous click.

She spun around, gasping for the breath he had knocked out of her even before she knew where he was going with that cryptic statement. She only knew it was bad.

"Like *what*?" she asked.

His hand was in a fist against his thigh. "We don't have to marry now."

It took her a few moments to find words—her ears were ringing so badly.

"Was it always about *having* to and never about *wanting* to?" she managed to ask.

"Yes." He was utterly still, his profile carved from granite. "If I had to marry, I thought it should be you." He swallowed loud enough for her to hear it. "But I'm realizing how self-serving that was. I didn't recognize how many pitfalls there were for you. This is your chance to walk away before any real damage is done."

Her heart being in tatters notwithstanding?

"You're going to put that on me?" she asked, pressing her hand between her breasts. "I can walk away if *I* want to?" What happened to committing in good faith?

"No," he stated flatly. "I'm going to tell you to go. You'll be better off," he had the nerve to proclaim.

"How does that compute?" she asked, voice husked by gall.

He closed his eyes as though suffering something unbearable. "You don't want to marry me, Sopi. You never did."

"No, *you* don't want to marry *me*," she flung at him. "*I love you.* I would want to marry you if you wanted me, but you *don't*. Is it because I didn't—"

"Don't finish that sentence," he cut in sharply, speaking through his teeth. A muscle pulsed in his jaw. "But that's part of why

I'm doing this. It's one thing for a couple to want children and discover they can't make it happen. This damned title puts far too much demand on you to perform. I can't put that on you. Not when I saw how much it hurt you when..." He lifted a helpless hand.

She didn't tell him she could live with that sort of pressure if he loved her. He didn't contradict her on not wanting to marry her, though—which was probably the cruelest thing anyone had ever done to her.

He broke the charged silence by drawing in a deep breath. "I'll make arrangements for you to travel back to Canada."

"Don't bother," she said flatly, no longer the doormat who allowed lesser people than him to walk all over her. "Thanks to you, I have resources of my own." A house in Sweden, for instance.

"I know it doesn't seem like I'm thinking of you, but I am," he said gravely.

"No, you're not!" She really ought to be grateful to him for all he'd done, but she was too angry. "You're doing this because you like *pain*. I don't understand why you feel a need to punish yourself, but fine. I'll lean into it and be the point of agony you need. You're welcome."

CHAPTER TEN

THE FINAL FLIP of Sopi's magnificent hair as she had walked out on him might as well have been a bullwhip that continued to flay him over the ensuing days.

It stung especially deep when he informed his brother and Elise that she was gone. They both stared at him with exasperation and bewilderment.

"But I liked her," Elise protested in an injured tone. "What if the next woman you choose isn't…her?"

Rhys hadn't thought that far ahead. Now the remark was salt in a wound, rubbing and rubbing. Henrik might have an heir on the way, but more children were next to impossible for them. Rhys would still have to marry and make a few spares.

The idea of lying with anyone but Sopi made him sick.

He buried himself in work, trying not to

think of her, trying not to let Sopi's absence cause more work to fall on Elise. As for Henrik, Rhys had to stay ahead of him or he would stubbornly refuse to rest.

"You're starting to look sicker than I am. Walk with me," Henrik commanded one morning. He was home again for the weekend, and spring sunshine was breaking through the breakfast room window.

They were no sooner on the path along the lakeshore, a refreshing breeze skating across the lake, when Henrik said, "What do you plan to do about Sopi?"

"Nothing. We called it off."

"Why? And don't give me your fabrications about things not working out. You didn't have to convince me she was right for you. I saw it with my own eyes, only for you to turn around and tell me you were mistaken. You're never wrong," Henrik said drily. "In fact, I don't think you were acting. I think you genuinely love her."

He loved her so much he couldn't breathe for missing her. She had only been in his bed a few short weeks and he reached for her in the dark every night. When he heard a footstep in the lounge, his heart leaped in anticipation. When Elise had a light spell of morning sickness, he wondered how Sopi would have coped.

He wondered if she would have children with someone else and wondered how he would make his own when he only wanted one woman in this world.

They had arrived on the end of the floating wharf, rebuilt three years ago, but in the same spot where they had climbed aboard a rowboat with the servants two decades ago.

"I do love her." A weight came off his chest as he admitted it out loud for the first time.

"Then go get her, you idiot."

He wanted to. He was barely surviving exactly the sort of loss he had feared when he pushed her away, but cowardice wasn't the only thing that had driven him that day.

"I haven't been coping well with your diagnosis, Henrik. I keep thinking it should be me going through this, not you."

"Don't," Henrik growled.

"*I* was the one who tried to attack the guard." His voice had roots in the horror of *that night*.

"You were a child," Henrik said quietly. "Terrified and reacting in the moment. You can't blame yourself for actions taken by monsters. It took Elise a long time to convince me that my responsibility was for the future of Verina, not its past. Yours, too. We can strive to maintain peace and ensure Verina prospers, Rhys. We can't undo what has already happened."

"I still think... I cost us *them*. Cost *you*. My actions pushed you into all of this long before you were old enough to handle it. You deserve to be happy, Henrik. You've fought so hard for everything. The crown, Elise, a baby. Now you're fighting for your life. I couldn't stomach the fact that everything you have had to struggle so hard for had just fallen into my lap. A woman I love who has a title?" He laughed drily. "For a few days, we thought she was pregnant, and I was so..." He looked into the sun to try to burn back the wetness in his eyes. "I couldn't accept how happy I was. How easily all of that happiness had come to me."

"So you pushed her away to punish yourself? What happens if you have to take the throne? Will you marry someone you hate just so you can feel truly miserable?"

"I don't want to think of it, Henrik." His heart was being crushed in a thorny vise. "I don't want the throne. I want my brother, alive and well."

"Well, today is your lucky day. I'm here. And I'm going to be a good brother and tell you that I want you to be happy. Not pin-headed." He frowned with impatience. "Don't you dare martyr yourself and expect me to praise you for it. Yes, love demands sacrifice. More often, it gives us the strength to crawl through hell and come out the other side. How do you think I got through those early years? How do you think I got out of this palace that night? *You.* I would have died here if I hadn't been so determined to get you out alive."

Rhys's heart lurched, and he swallowed, but the lump in his throat remained. "I felt like a responsibility back then. A weight." That was why he'd worked so hard to ensure they got ahead. "I've always wanted to make up for that somehow."

"And that's what Sopi is? Your payment?"

He snorted at the twisted logic. "This will come as a shock, Rhys, but you are not a god. You cannot influence the outcome of what I face. All this hurt you're causing yourself and Sopi achieves nothing."

He was starting to realize that.

"But maybe you're right to let her go. Let her find someone who will love her the way she deserves to be loved."

Rhys snapped his brother a glower.

"Oh, did that sting?" Henrik taunted. "Good."

"You're lucky I'm in a hurry or I'd push you into the lake," Rhys muttered.

He took out his phone as he strode into the palace, dialing for Gerard—who had a standing order to stay in touch with Sopi in case she needed anything.

Or, as the case was right now, Rhys needed *her*.

The caretaker of the Basile-Munier "cottage" was actually a penny-pinching widower who welcomed Sopi with a warm hug. He lived with his daughter in the village and came up daily to garden and check on the place.

The house was, in reality, a mansion of two stories with turrets on either end. It faced the azure water of a fjord and had a cobbled driveway surrounded by natural forest. The cream-colored siding, green tin roof and gingerbread rickrack made it look like a white cake with spearmint frosting. Sopi adored it, especially after she filled the half-barrel tubs with geraniums and discovered the path down the slope to the village.

She had meant to stay only a few days to lick her wounds, but she was thinking of lingering until the midsummer festival. The baristas in the village had told her the sun would set behind the mountains, but only for an hour. Most people stayed up to watch it set and rise, enjoying dancing and food, drinking and song for a solid twenty-four hours.

Hopefully there would be some forgetting among all that.

Sighing wistfully, she climbed past the abandoned house with the sod roof, always inspired by the resilience it symbolized. People had lived there once. They had dug into the hillside and hibernated through the long winters, probably with a half dozen children underfoot.

People survived the most amazing things. She could survive this heartbreak.

Ah. There was a different wildflower. She bent to pluck it. The barista had told her one of the festival traditions was for young women to pick a bouquet of seven different flowers. If she put them under her pillow, her future husband would appear in a dream.

Sopi had a daisy and some clover and what looked like a buttercup. She didn't know the name of anything else she'd found. There was a cluster of delicate pink things with serrated petals and what she thought was thistle, so she had wrapped a tissue around the stem. Now these little crimson things were dangling off a drooping stem like bleeding hearts.

How apropos. Oh. And forget-me-nots, she noted wryly, stooping to pluck a few. That made seven and a rather sorry-looking bouquet, but desperate times.

Adjusting her shopping bag on her shoulder and her sun hat on her head, she finished the steep ascent to the small lawn and the patio where she ate every evening until the mosquitos chased her inside.

"Oh." She halted and the tissue-wrapped bouquet dropped to the grass. Yearning coiled around her, squeezing the air from her lungs.

Rhys sat in one chair and had his feet propped on another. Watchful.

"What are you doing here?" she asked, bracing herself.

"The house was locked. Your cell service is terrible. I've been trying to guess your Wi-Fi." He set aside his phone.

She almost told him it was MoreFishInThe-Sea, but admitted, "It's one of those nonsensical things with dashes and mixed caps."

She set her bag on the table to dig for her keys and hide her anxiety at him showing up out of the blue like this. "How are Henrik and Elise?"

"Fine."

He wasn't bringing bad news, then. That was good, she supposed, but her tension remained, wondering why he was here. She unlocked the back door, and he came into the kitchen with her.

"This is beautiful." He moved across the

open space to the lounge, where the big picture windows looked onto the sloping lawn, the village below and the sparkling fjord winding around a bend in the distance.

"Thank you. I'm having trouble leaving." She loved it rather desperately, maybe for the connection to her mother that it was. She moved to put away her handful of groceries, then poured two lemonades. "I can see why my mother wanted Cassiopeia's. It must have made her feel at home."

He nodded and glanced at the view again, hiding his thoughts.

She set her hat on a stool, then brought the glasses over.

"Thank you," he murmured absently, swinging his gaze back to her as he took the glass. Whatever preoccupying thoughts had been in his face creased into a scowl. "Damn it, Sopi, it's been *nine days*."

"Oh." She touched the hair cropped to chin length. "The salon in the village does that thing where they donate hair to kids with cancer." And she'd been *mad*.

She turned to look at the view. Sipped. Felt him blistering her profile with his hot stare.

Goodness, that was satisfying, even though her heart was still raw.

"See, if you were still my lover, I might have consulted you," she dared to taunt. "But you aren't. Would you like to sit outside?" she asked politely. "There's usually a nice breeze."

"The irony is, Sopi," he said through gritted teeth, "I love you most when you're digging in your heels and standing up for yourself. I'm going to hold a grudge about this for a long time. Probably until it grows back, but I love you for doing whatever the hell you want."

She wanted to say something pithy, but her vision blurred. She frowned at the smeared vision of green and blue beyond the windows. Bit a lip that began to tremble.

"What am I supposed to say to that, Rhys?" Her voice was barely a wisp.

"You could say you'll marry me."

"You'll forgive me if I don't leap on that offer *again*." She moved to set aside her glass before she dropped it.

"Tell me to go to hell, then. I deserve it." His glass also went onto a side table. He cupped her face and made her look at him. "You were right. I thought I needed to suffer. I have."

"Why?"

"Because I didn't know how to be happy. Not like that. Not without feeling guilty for it. I was so disappointed that you weren't pregnant, Sopi. So crushed. I don't know how I'll function if we have trouble conceiving. There, I've admitted it. I'm not impervious. I hurt and fear and damn well need you beside me or I can't bear the uncertainties of life."

Each husky word took strips off her heart.

"And I didn't want a baby because I needed an heir. I wanted a baby with *you*. The one that would make us into a little family of our own. But I couldn't accept that desire in me without feeling I was stealing something from Henrik. From people who don't have *this*."

He didn't have to tell her what *this* was. She felt it as a sparkling force field around them. One that made her feel as though she floated four feet above the ground.

"And now?" she asked in a thready whisper, eyes dampening.

"Now I know that living without you is

more punishment than people are meant to withstand."

"It felt like you were punishing me. That you didn't want me to be happy. That no one does."

"I know." His expression was agonized, but he gave a little tug to the tendril of hair dangling against her jaw. "But this tells me that you will go after your own happiness somehow, someway. And I hope that means you'll take another chance that I can give you the happiness you deserve."

Her mouth trembled as she wavered.

"This time you know exactly what you're getting," he coaxed. "You know you're my equal. That I want *you*. Because *I love you*."

Her tears brimmed. "I love you, too. A *lot*."

"Thank God," he breathed and caught her as she threw herself into his arms.

Their first kiss was hard, but tender. Apology and reunion, but it slid quickly toward passion until they were practically consuming one another.

He let out a growl and scooped up to cradle her against his chest. "Where's the bedroom?"

She pointed at the stairs.

"Hell, no. I'll save my strength for more important things." He set her on the sofa and joined her, covering her laughter with a kiss.

EPILOGUE

Cassiopeia's Spa and Retreat,
Canada, six years later

RHYS WAS IN his robe, waiting for his wife, but he quickly discovered she had left their suite. His bodyguard said something about ice cream, and Rhys went down to the darkened dining room and through to the kitchen that had been closed for the night.

"*Süsse*, I thought you were changing?" He didn't mention the pool or they would have company for sure.

"I went to say good-night and was reminded of a promise I'd made." She wore her evening gown and the anniversary diamonds Rhys had given her before they had come away on this business vacation, but she dug the ice cream scoop into the bucket herself, handing cones to each of their three children.

"Will you take a picture of me, Daddy? I

want to show Reggie," their eldest, Sarah, asked. She was third in line for the throne after Rhys and her cousin, Reginald. Fortunately, none of them were worrying about taking Henrik's position anytime soon. He'd been pronounced fully in remission last month.

Even so, the early years of a family drawn close by health challenges had made Sarah and Reggie almost like twins. They were close in age, temperament and intelligence and missed each other terribly if they were away from each other more than a day or two. Rhys found it endearing and hoped they never grew out of it.

"It's bubberscutch," Robbie said, getting some on his nose with his first lick. He grinned, always their entertainer.

Rhys wiped the ice cream away with his fingertip, chuckling and dropping an affectionate kiss on his son's messy hair.

"Maybe you could share one with Marcus?" Sopi suggested as their baby held out a hand and said, "Pea?"

Rhys took fifteen-month-old Marcus from the nanny. He'd been a surprise, and there'd never been a more welcome one. Rhys loved all his children so much, he thought he would burst.

And then there was his wife. Sopi made cones for the nannies, then one for herself before she returned the bucket to the freezer and dropped the scoop into the dish pit.

"You've come a long way, Princess," he teased as she rejoined them.

"Right?" She chuckled. "I didn't want to call the chef back just for this." Her tongue swirled along the edge of her cone.

He had plans for that tongue. First, however, they had to get their children back into their room and their beds, if not actually asleep.

"We'll all go swimming *in the morning*," Rhys promised a short while later when they had everyone abed.

He quickly whisked his wife down to the treatment level.

"I was going to put on a bathing suit," she protested.

"Why? You won't be wearing anything for long." He collected a spare robe and towels—he learned from his mistakes—

and they slipped out the door into the falling snow.

Snickering like conspirators, they made their way through the dark to the private hot pool that was more than a source of healing, magical waters. It was a return to the place where they'd fallen in love. They quickly stripped naked and immersed themselves in its warm embrace.

* * * * *